"Business is the only thing between us," Misha said resolutely.

"Is it?"

Misha knew Talib was right behind her without needing to look back and prove it to herself.

"Is it, Misha?" The back of his hand trailed the curve of her spine. His finger curled into the belt around her robe in case she had any thoughts of moving away.

Talib spun Misha around gracefully and placed his mouth on hers. Her tongue thrust eagerly against his, giving just as much fire as he gave. She was so absorbed in the kiss that she hardly noticed him lifting her up against his body and carrying her in the direction of the bedroom.

Finding her nude beneath the robe, Talib took full advantage. He kissed his way down Misha's neck and up again, almost painfully aroused by the supple curves on her slender body. Her bottom was full and molded perfectly to his palms when he cupped them. Her breasts were firm, flawlessly rounded mounds that beckoned his lips, teeth and tongue.

Having had his fill of kissing for the moment, he ventured lower.

Books by AlTonya Washington

Kimani Romance

A Lover's Pretense
A Lover's Mask
Pride and Consequence
Rival's Desire
Hudson's Crossing
The Doctor's Private Visit
As Good as the First Time

Kimani Arabesque

Remember Love
Guarded Love
Finding Love Again
Love Scheme
A Lover's Dream

ALTONYA WASHINGTON

wears many titles. Aside from Mom, her favorite is romance author. Crafting stories and characters that are sexy and engaging with a fair amount of mystery really keeps her busy. When AlTonya's not writing, she works as a library assistant and as social secretary to an active son—a job that demands the bulk of her time.

Every CHANCE *I Get*

ALTONYA WASHINGTON

To the readers who wanted more Talib. Here he is!

 KIMANI PRESS™

Recycling programs
for this product may
not exist in your area.

ISBN-13: 978-0-373-86198-9

EVERY CHANCE I GET

Copyright © 2011 by AlTonya Washington

www.kimanipress.com

Printed in U.S.A.

Dear Reader,

This is the book so many of you have been asking for. Since his appearance in *Hudson's Crossing,* many of you have been captivated by my sexy Brit, Talib Mason. The history between him and our heroine, Misha Bales, has simmered in a sea of unrest for far too long. It's time for their attraction to be confronted and conquered.

Readers have asked why I chose to make Talib British, and plenty of others have told me just how happy they are about it. It was actually quite exciting to craft another non-American hero, which I've done before in other stories. And like before, I've had the best time with everything, from the speech patterns and language to the more alluring elements that lurk seductively below the surface of his British persona.

Let's find out if Misha can hold her own against a man as delectable as Talib.

Be sure to let me know what you think. Email me at altonya@lovealtonya.com and visit my website, www.lovealtonya.com.

Best,

AlTonya

To the Romance Slam Jam organizers and participants,
the book clubs and the LoveAlTonya webgroup.
You all have been such a phenomenal force in my career
in so many ways. I wish you continued success
in all your individual endeavors.
I feel honored and blessed by your support.

Prologue

August 2005
New York

Talib Mason planned on finding a ticket plastered to his windshield by the time he returned to the parking lot. He didn't give a damn, of course. So what if he parked on the curb and dangerously close to a fire hydrant? He'd already done well enough to reach his destination without wrecking the car along the way.

He'd spent the better part of the day cursing himself for letting the argument with Misha get so far out of hand. He slammed the elevator button with his fist. To accuse her had been unfair. That story could have only been leaked by someone with inside knowledge. But he had accused *her*, and he'd been at his cruelest while he'd done it. The things he'd said…

It felt like his heart was about to crush his ribs. It'd been pounding viciously ever since he'd spoken with her assistant.

At that time of night, the corridors of St. Joseph's Hospital were almost completely silent. The third-shift nurses were either making rounds or engaged in light conversation while gathered around their station. Conversation ceased, though, when the four women at the nurses' station caught sight of the man who rushed from the elevator and bounded toward them. The fact that he appeared as provocative as sin did nothing to mask the outrage darkening his expression.

"Misha Bales." Added to his dark expression was the abrupt tone in his voice. The tone was unavoidable, given his fear that he was about to lose her. The usually seductive level of his British-laced brogue came across as harsh and dangerous.

Given the circumstances, the nurses were hesitant to release any information. They exchanged uncertain glances. This did nothing to soothe Talib's temper, already teetering close to the edge of explosion. Silently he warred with himself, gripping the edge of the counter as he bowed his head. Security was but a button's push away as he was sure the nurses were well aware. Thankfully, the world wasn't completely against him.

"Talib? Talib, is that you?"

He heard his name and saw Dr. Lettia Breene approaching the station.

The lovely full-figured obstetrician wore a concerned frown as she could all but feel the tension in the air. "I hope you're here for a checkup." She took note of his haggard appearance, then asked the nurses, "What's going on?"

Talib responded first. "Misha's here, Lett."

"Misha?" Lettia turned back toward the nurses.

RN Connie Wesley checked a book on the desk and nodded. "Car accident, Dr. B." She looked toward her colleagues who were all nodding.

"It was about four hours ago," Nurse Adrian White added and passed Lett the report on Misha. "The EMTs said she had to be pried out of the car."

"Jesus," Talib moaned.

Lett set aside the chart and put a hand on his shoulder. "What room is she in?"

Minutes later, Talib was being directed toward the unit where Misha was being treated. The six-foot-plus former linebacker had to lean on the doctor when he saw Misha bandaged and resting in the dim room.

"God," Lettia whispered. She was just as devastated as Talib was, shaking her head slowly in disbelief.

"It's my fault." Emotion had rendered Talib's voice raw.

"Shh…" Lettia rubbed his back. "Honey, blaming yourself won't do either of you any good."

"It's my fault."

"Talib—"

"Don't tell her I was here."

"But, Talib, she'll—"

"Swear it, Lett."

"Honey, why?"

"Just swear it, Lettia."

She nodded, even as she searched his face in wonder. "All right," she said when he took her shoulders.

Satisfied, he turned back to Misha. She was already uncommonly small and the bed she occupied looked gargantuan with her in the middle of it.

"Will she…be okay?" His voice wavered while he brushed his thumb across the bruises darkening her jaw and cheek.

Lettia nodded, easing a hand into the pocket of her white coat. "From what I read in the chart, everything points toward her making a full recovery. It's gonna take time though. She banged herself up pretty badly."

Talib leaned in close to study Misha intently, as if he were trying to memorize her features—battered as they were.

"Remember, you swore not to tell her I came here."

"Tal—"

"Lettia."

"I won't."

Gingerly, Talib kissed an uninjured area on Misha's forehead. "I love you," he whispered against her skin, and then left the room.

"Tal…Tal? Talib…" Misha was stirring mere seconds after the door closed.

Lettia glanced over her shoulder, debating on whether to go after Talib. Instinct told her that a line had been crossed between the couple and it was best to let things be.

"Talib...I...I'm sorry."

"Honey, shhh..." Lettia spoke near her friend's ear.

Misha rolled her head slowly across the pillow. She frowned, trying to open eyes that were swollen shut.

Lettia pressed a hand to her hair. "Shh...honey you need to rest. Shh..."

"He has to know I'm sorry. He has to know it...." Her words could barely be heard as they tripped past her bruised lips.

Lettia kissed the spot Talib had earlier. "He does, hon. He does."

Chapter 1

Present Day

Asher and Riley Hudson's Bedford home swelled with talk and laughter. Guests filled practically every room of the lovely two-story Southwestern styled house. People were still arriving, their vehicles circling around as drivers searched for parking space on the stadium-size lawn.

The guest list may have been a tad lengthy for a baptism, but no one wanted to miss out on the chance to meet the newest and cutest Hudson. The fact that a baby was the guest of honor put all parents in attendance at ease. No one had to search for a sitter since all kids were welcome. The younger children had a wonderful time breaking in Ahmad Hudson's elaborate playground set while the older ones enjoyed several rounds of basketball on the two courts the property boasted. For adults and kids alike, the gathering was a sheer delight.

Happiness loomed over everyone. Everyone, that is, except the guest of honor's godparents. Thankfully, a fair share of business-talk intermingled with the afternoon's events, occupying Talib and Misha just enough to keep their thoughts and eyes off one another.

Such was the case when Misha stood near the bar cooing with her godson/nephew and nuzzling her nose to his cheek.

"Already got the man buyin' you drinks, huh?"

Misha laughed at Tony Geraldson's remark and gave the baby a tiny bounce. "A woman's gotta train a man early," she told the heavy-set bartender.

Tony laughed when the five-month-old in Misha's arms cooed as though he were voicing his opinion on the matter. Misha's dark eyes glinted merrily but she tilted her head when it appeared the baby was looking elsewhere. Turning, she discovered what had sparked the child's cheerful outburst.

"Talib." Her glee vanished.

"Misha." His voice was soft. "You need help here?" He was already leaning close to tickle his nephew's cheek.

Misha bristled when the scent of his cologne teased her nostrils. "We're good." Her voice was tight yet her expression softened when she looked back down at the baby.

It was easy for Talib to take note of the vinegar in

her voice and he smiled. Knowing he was playing with fire, he moved a tad closer. "Shouldn't you ease up a bit?" His dark gaze spanned the length of the bar.

"Counting my visits?" She rolled her eyes. "Could you hurry with that *ginger ale,* Tony?"

"Got it right here, Misha."

She turned and gently set Ahmad in his uncle's arms. Without another word, she took her drink and stormed off.

Talib pressed a kiss to Ahmad's forehead and watched Misha disappear into the crowd. "Now I've done it, haven't I, mate?" He chuckled as the baby seemed to coo in agreement.

"What the hell do you mean, you're sorry?" Misha had bolted away from Talib only to have her temper freshly stoked when her best friend forbid her to leave.

Riley cringed and waved her hand to ward off Misha's frustration. "I hope you don't whine like that around Ahmad. 'Cause I'll bring him over for *you* to deal with if he ever starts it."

Misha folded her arms over the draping bodice of her dress. "Well, I'll be happy to take him home with me right now. I just can't stand to be here for another minute. No offense."

"Mmm-hmm." Riley didn't veer from her task of adding more hors d'oeuvres to a platter while lecturing Misha at the same time. "And is it the party or Talib you're running away from?"

"Oh come on now, Riley." Misha reached over to swipe two of the goat-cheese pastries from the platter. "You know, this is some thanks I get after all my understanding about you and Asher."

"Dammit," Riley hissed, almost cutting her finger upon listening to Misha. "Right. Understanding. Well, if understanding means feeling kicked around by your best friend, then I guess you were tremendously understanding."

"Motherhood has made you cold." Misha's tone was matter-of-fact.

Riley finally took pity and turned to cup her friend's face. "What's this really about?"

Misha pulled Riley's hands away. "It's really about him being *here*. Him being back in my life, so to speak, after six years when he's supposed to be back in Phoenix. Even if it is just temporary."

"Right." Riley puffed her cheeks nervously and turned back to the goat cheese spread.

"Hold it." Misha grabbed Riley by the chain belt at her waist. "Spill it."

"I really need to get this stuff out—"

"Riley!"

"All right!" She set the knife on the counter. "Well, you already know he's here helping Asher with the new office."

"Right. And?"

"*And*…he may be here awhile."

"What's 'a while'? Weeks?" she probed when Riley

wasn't forthcoming with an answer. "Months? *Months,* Riley?"

"Oh, stop it, please." Riley propped a hand to her hip. "You knew this wasn't something that could be done overnight."

"Just tell me he's definitely going back to Phoenix and not moving out here." Misha leaned against the counter and rested her face in her hands. She looked up when Riley didn't respond right away.

"He's definitely going back to Phoenix and not moving out here."

"Humph." Misha's lashes fluttered as she rolled her eyes. "I'd be better off asking Asher."

"Ha! Like he'd tell you anything Talib asked him not to. Those two are thick as thieves." Riley shrugged and turned back to the platter. "I used to think *we* were thick as thieves."

"What are you talking about?" Misha's tone was absent as she worried over Talib's next move.

Riley tucked a clipped lock of her hair behind her ear and grimaced. "When are you gonna share the real and full story on you and Talib?"

Misha stopped biting her thumbnail and frowned at her friend.

"I know there's more you haven't told me."

"What more is there to tell? You know the messiest part of it all."

"That you went down an ugly road." Riley went to put the spread back inside the refrigerator. "That's all you told me and to this day I've got no idea what that means."

"Jeez, Riley, do you need me to spell it out for you?"

"Yes. You bet I do when I see you this way. Running from a man isn't something you do. I've seen you pounce a lot of brothers but never run from them."

Misha's wrapped hair covered her face more fully when she bowed her head again. "They weren't Talib."

"Will you promise to come and talk to me if you need it?" Riley decided against putting on more pressure and extended her hands.

Misha accepted the offer and kissed her friend's cheek before they hugged.

"This is the most important thing anyone will ever tell you, man. *Fumble* is the worst word in the English language."

Talib and Ahmad were catching the last quarter of a pre-season football game while they relaxed in the den. Talib occupied one of the deep suede armchairs and propped his feet up on an ottoman. Ahmad was beginning to doze from his cozy position near his uncle's chest.

"What's goin' on, fellas?" Asher greeted when he found the two camped out before the television. "What's the score?" He tickled Ahmad's cheek then chose a spot on the other armchair.

"Twenty-eight, twenty-one. Not in our favor," Talib announced.

"How's Wade?" Asher referred to one of their newest clients, Nevil Wade.

"Sharp as usual, but the bloke can't do much with the so-called help he's got."

Business consumed the conversation for several moments. In the midst of it, Talib kissed his nephew's head and passed him over to his dad.

"So why're you holed up in here?" Asher queried when a commercial broke into the game. "Tons of people out there are wanting a second of your time." He tossed his tie over his shoulder and settled in more comfortably with Ahmad. "I'd appreciate the truth," he tacked on. Seconds passed before he accepted there would be no response from his friend. "You and Misha avoiding each other when you want to be right next to each other…seems pretty stupid."

"I've been considering more exposure for the new branch." Talib slipped his feet back into the polished tan wing tips he'd been sporting.

"Are you crazy? We've been getting exposure left and right."

"Print exposure."

Asher smiled. "What have you got in mind?"

The look Talib slanted was answer enough.

"Hell, man, why don't you just go and talk to her?"

"That's all I want." Talib stood and walked over to lean against the tall pine bar in the room. "But she wants no part of it—of me."

"That's a lie, you know." Asher's voice was light as he nuzzled his son's hair.

"I'm not so sure it is, Ash." Talib studied the invisible pattern his index finger traced into the bar top. "She's more than angry with me. I suspected it before, but now I know."

Concern shadowed Asher's light eyes. "You know what?"

"She's terrified."

"Of you?"

"I think so. No, no, that's not right." Talib pushed off the bar and strolled the room. He stroked the silky whiskers darkening the honey tone of his face. "No, I don't think she's terrified. I'm bloody sure as hell of it."

Misha found solace on a secluded bend along the back porch. She wiggled to a more comfortable position on a cushioned seat and heard a crinkle from the paper she accidentally sat on. She smiled, finding several outdated newspapers belonging to their competition. Silently, she commended Riley's thoroughness. The girl always liked to see what the other guy was doing, so she could take it one step further—one step better. Despite that, Misha felt her approval waning when she saw a copy of *The First Beacon*.

Misha placed aside her disgust and browsed the paper. But it just returned full steam when she saw that the *Beacon* had added a new section to the paper.

That week's edition boasted the debut of "The Word on Entertainment" by editor Justine Duke.

"That shady wench." Misha seethed with anger as she conjured the image of her former colleague and greatest enemy. The woman's irresponsible reporting had caused several upsets between Riley and Asher. Not to mention the upsets between Misha and Talib.

Misha felt her anger gradually taper into anticipation. The need for a slice of revenge was rising sure and steady.

"There you are!" Gloria Reynolds's firm voice filled the area when she waltzed around the corner. "I've been looking everywhere for you."

"Well, you found me." Misha made room on the lounge chair and watched as Gloria angled her tall, curvy frame next to her.

"The baby's baptism is turning out to be the biggest business party of the season."

Misha had to laugh at the woman's excitement. "I'll bet you've got enough scoops to keep *The New Chronicle* thick for the next year."

"I won't deny that." Gloria gave a quick toss of her auburn locks. "But it's not *The New Chronicle* I've collected the biggest scoop for, but *The Stamper Court*." She spoke of the new publication Riley had been slated to run with Misha as her chief editor.

Intrigued, Misha sat up a bit straighter on the lounge chair listening as Gloria talked of a feature on Hud-Mason.

"We've already got Asher's and Talib's blessings to

run with the thing. The co-owners are eager for as much exposure as possible."

Misha knew that wouldn't be difficult for them to obtain. Talk of the successful agents was everywhere. Even the advertising world had caught the fever. Talib's and Asher's faces were gracing everything from NYC subways to billboards in Times Square.

Misha noted that an exposé would be great for her and Riley's new publication which was garnering almost as much talk as Talib's and Asher's new venture.

"Are we talking more of a background piece or something more specialized?"

Gloria bit her thumbnail and considered the question. "Oh, this would definitely be more specialized."

Misha reached for her phone to input notes, but realized she'd left it in the baby's nursery when she first arrived at the party. "Well, I can put Coyt Parsons on it." She ran down the project in her head. "He'd love the opportunity. He certainly does have a flair for flashy writing and this would probably call for just that."

"You may want to wait on that." Gloria scooted to the edge of the lounge. "The board is gonna insist on you handling it."

"Why?" Misha moved to the edge of the lounge, as well. "I'm an editor, Gloria, not a writer. Trust me, I know my limits."

"That may be, but you writing the story was the one thing they insisted on."

"Right." Misha leaned back and regarded her publisher with clear suspicion in her tilting onyx stare.

"Is this what Riley and me are gonna have to look forward to with our new publication? Will the brass always *insist* on how we should handle our stories?"

Gloria was about to respond, when she paused and looked past Misha. "Not *our* brass, hon." She patted her hand to Misha's knee and stood.

Misha followed the direction of the woman's gaze to Talib Mason.

Chapter 2

"Talib," Gloria greeted the man with a nod and soft smile. She hurried from the porch, tuning into the fact that war was in the air.

"What are you doing?" Suspicion all but blazed from Misha's eyes.

When he approached, she retreated. Talib noticed and it triggered his frustration anew. He moved forward until he'd invaded her personal space quite adequately.

"When would you like to start meeting to discuss the story?"

Misha attempted to make a move around him, but he wouldn't allow it.

"I can send someone out first thing on Monday," she said.

Talib slipped a hand into a side pocket of his cream

trousers and bowed his head. "Gloria did tell you we expect your personal attention on this, didn't she?"

"Do you realize that I'm a very busy woman?" She blinked hair from her eyes so he could see the full extent of her emotion. "I don't have to be involved in every stage of research to write this story, you know?"

"For this story, you do. Take it or leave it."

Her smile was sweet. "I'll leave it."

He stepped aside when she tried to move past him that time.

"Your bosses aren't going to like that you walked out on one of the biggest stories of the year."

"Spare me, Talib. You and Asher are everywhere. I'm sure the world knows all about the two former ballers making yet another splash in the agenting world they already rule."

Talib took a seat on the porch railing. "No one else has this part of the story—the background on who we are—who we *really* are."

Curiosity winning out over suspicion, Misha walked toward him. "Exactly what is your intention for this feature?"

"What time may I expect you on Monday?"

Misha muttered under her breath and attempted to control her temper. "Don't for a second think you can rile me in my own business. I don't know yet what you're trying to do—"

"Trying to do, love? I'm trying to give you a story."

"Mmm-hmm, I know what you're trying to give me, Tali."

"Is that so?" She was close enough to touch and he took advantage. "Why do you keep running from me, then?"

Misha didn't try to twist out of the grip he had on her forearm. Patiently, she waited for him to release her but discovered too late that he had more in mind first.

The kiss and caress that followed wasn't forced. Misha leaned into it willingly, needingly. Talib loosened his hold on her arm the instant their lips met. He didn't move from the rail and only began to caress her when she moved closer. Her hair brushed his hands when he massaged her back and shoulders. Whimpering sounds vibrated from both of them while their tongues fought a slow duel. Misha raked the silky curls tapered at Talib's neck and arched closer into the powerful wall of his chest.

Reluctantly, Talib acknowledged that he'd have to be the one to end things. He'd take her right there against the rail if he didn't let her go soon. Breaking the kiss smoothly, he let his mouth trail her neck.

"So when may I expect you on Monday?"

The words, no matter the elegant tone they were delivered in, were like a cold splash. Misha twisted away from him.

"I'll call you." For the second time that afternoon, she stormed away from him.

Talib's cool expression merged into one less certain. Slumping on the railing, he prayed this plan of his would have a chance at actually working.

* * *

"What's Talib done now?" Riley drawled while setting her baby's stuffed animals to a far corner of the crib.

"Why don't we talk about how long *you've* known about Justine Duke's new publication."

Riley's hands paused on the toys. "You know I always keep up with the competition."

"But you had to know I'd be interested in something like that. Why wouldn't you tell me?"

"Because I didn't want you flying off the deep end about the woman. You almost lost your mind over the crap she pulled before and with your history…"

"Riley, please, you've got no idea about our *history*."

Riley made sure the baby's monitor was on, then firmly ushered Misha into her bedroom which was connected to the nursery.

"I need my phone," Misha said, remembering.

"It's already on the nightstand." Riley motioned for Misha to sit down on the bed next to her. "Talk."

"What—" Misha spread her hands "—is this about, Justine?"

"This is about you telling me the rest of what happened. Now."

"We… Justine and I worked together before—"

"Hell, Misha, I know all that."

Wearily, Misha leaned forward, resting her elbows to her knees. "There was a client…Talib and Asher were preparing to sign him. They were just starting up the agency. Talib had been in town wooing clients while Asher was still setting up shop in Phoenix."

Riley got up and moved over to sit on the vanity stool before her dresser and listened.

"Anyway, the guy they were going after the hardest… he was a real jerk. Nothing like Vic," she said, referring to *The New Chronicle*'s former fact-checker and Hud-Mason's newest client, Victor Lyne. "Ray Simmons was his name. I got to meet him a few times at some parties Talib took me to. That was enough to tell me that the guy was just in it for the money. At the time, me and Justine were both working for *The First Beacon*." She shrugged and curled against a pillow lining the headboard.

"We were good colleagues. Not friends, but good enough coworkers to feel comfortable bouncing ideas off one another. There was the occasional chatter about men and dates. I told her about Talib, meeting his new client and how money hungry the guy was." Misha leaned back and folded her arms across her chest. "Justine was trying to make a splash with her entertainment features even back then. She was a so-so writer, looked down on being an assistant when what she really wanted were full-fledged reporting creds. She figured Ray Simmons was just the ticket. So she wrote a splashy story on the guy and got the paper to run it because he had connections to the up-and-coming Hud-Mason agency. Humph, Hud-Mason never had the chance to sign him. Justine's story revealed that Ray held no loyalties to anyone—he was going with whoever got him the biggest bucks. Another agency worked up a deal for him and scooped him right out from under Talib and Asher."

"Talib didn't take that too well, I guess."

Misha gave a mock salute in Riley's direction and closed her eyes on the memory.

"Men take betrayal far more seriously than women do. He was like someone I didn't know. He accused me…accused me in ways and of things… He said I'd slept with him for the story. It took days before I even knew what the hell he was talking about."

The despair in Misha's eyes tore at Riley's heart. She wanted to go to her, but resisted, knowing there was more to the story.

Absently, Misha fidgeted with the frame holding Asher and Riley's photo on one side and Ahmad's ultrasound on the other. Seconds passed before she swung her legs over the edge of the bed and raised the hem of her dress. She rubbed the scar at the bend of her knee.

"This won't ever heal, which is probably a good thing. That way I'll always have a reminder of—"

"The accident."

"Of *why* I had the accident."

"Misha—"

"I was completely out of it. Talib was the only thing on my mind. It's a wonder I knew where my keys were, let alone how to drive a car. I'm still amazed that I didn't kill myself."

Riley bristled then but knew she had to ask. "Is that what you were trying to do?"

"No. No." She spoke without hesitation and repeated the word when Riley stared. "I love living too much for that, but that night…me and Talib would've been together three years if that story hadn't broke. We met at a charity event. It was his third year in the league. I was there with someone from work. The guy couldn't dance worth a damn but it was a good networking opportunity. I'd just met someone from the *Beacon* and gotten an interview. I was even feeling good enough to risk my toes to a poor dance partner who twirled me right into Talib. His date was not thrilled."

Riley covered her mouth when she laughed.

Misha's amusement didn't last. "Three years later he couldn't stand my guts. That story came out and he wouldn't even give me the chance to explain. I saw him that day, tried one last time to talk—it didn't go well at all." She pounded a fist to the gray comforter. "None of this was my fault. Idle chatter with a coworker who took it and ran. I thought about that, getting madder and crazier every minute. Then I got in my car." She left the bed and walked to the windows overlooking the backyard.

Riley nodded, finally understanding her friend's real fear.

"I can't fall for him again." Misha turned her back on the windows. "Correction. I can't fall any deeper for him. If it fizzles again… What if the next time I get in my car…"

"Hey." Riley left the stool and came over to smooth her hands down Misha's arms. "You're smarter than that. Way too smart to let something like that dictate a decision not to have a future with the man you love."

"Talib doesn't love me." Misha shook her head, not willing to speak to the status of her own emotions then. "I don't know what he's up to, but it isn't about love."

"And how are you so sure?"

Misha flinched and turned back to the windows.

"So the question you have to answer is, why do you still want to keep Talib away?"

The party finally thinned out a couple of hours later. Riley insisted on Misha taking a nap in one of the guestrooms. When she woke, Misha decided to leave through the back and call later to let Riley know she was okay.

But leaving through the back was out of the question once she reached the garage and found her Acura blocked in by a black Navigator. She didn't have long to curse the driver, who arrived moments later.

"What the hell?" She waved toward the hulking vehicle.

"Slipping out through the back, what would our hosts say?" Talib chastised as he crossed the carved stone pavement.

"Move it, Talib."

"What time shall I expect you on Monday?"

"Didn't I say I'd call?"

He was standing over her so suddenly she hadn't even noticed he'd quickened his pace.

"It would be unwise for you to continue to play with me on this. I'm as busy as you are."

"Then you'll understand why I can't drop everything to come running when you command it."

His dimpled smile emerged then and he rubbed the material of her bodice between his thumb and forefinger. "I remember a time when you always *came running* for me."

The suggestion in his words had her leaning back on suddenly weak legs. "Well, I'm not that girl anymore."

He backed off, as well. "No, you're not that girl anymore. You're a high-powered editor whose bosses won't appreciate knowing we haven't even set up our first meeting."

"And you're a jackass."

"Then you should understand how uncomfortable I could make this for you, love."

"Is it really worth it, Talib? The agitation?"

"I, for one, don't see it as agitation. And yes, it's really worth it."

She watched him for a long moment and then stopped trying to figure him out. "Fine. Monday at ten."

He grinned. "Make it nine. You can treat me to breakfast."

"Talib, you—"

"I really like that place Red Sun." He was already striding off to move his car. He started the engine, backed out and left the truck idling while Misha fumed.

For the third, and what she hoped to be last time

for that day, she stormed off. She was frustrated that Talib convinced her to take the meeting and even more frustrated to admit to herself that she wanted to.

Chapter 3

Over a mug of coffee on Monday morning, Misha thought about all that had happened between her and Talib during the past several months. Going back any further than that was dangerous.

She stayed in for the remainder of the weekend following Ahmad's baptism party. She wouldn't call it cowardice. New York was a big place. It wasn't like she was going to run into Talib at every turn, for Pete's sake. Breakfast that morning would be more than enough "together time." Besides, she'd needed the rest of the weekend to mull over Riley's insights over her real resistance to Talib's sudden interest.

She wasn't afraid of a relapse but of something else she couldn't or wouldn't admit. What did that mean? She smirked into the coffee mug and berated herself.

Jeez, Misha, can't you even be honest with yourself in your own damn house?

What she couldn't or wouldn't admit was that she still loved him so very much that the emotion went far deeper than *falling* for someone. She loved and was in love with him as much as she'd been the day she'd cursed him and gone mad over the fact that he didn't believe in her.

There was more to that in-house admission, but before she could continue, the bell rang. She checked her watch, realized she wasn't wearing one and frowned when she noticed that the clock above the dining-room table read 7:35 a.m. *What the hell?*

"What the hell?" She uttered the phrase aloud when she opened the door to Talib. "It's 7:35 a.m."

"I thought I'd give you a lift."

"You know, regardless of my record, I can still handle a car, Talib."

He closed his eyes. "You know I didn't mean it that way."

"I know how you meant it. I'll see you there."

He wouldn't let her close the door. "And what sense does that make?"

"All the sense in the world, considering our breakfast appointment isn't until ten."

"*Nine,* remember?" He walked inside. "Besides, I thought you might like an idea of what we expect with this story."

"So *now* you want to talk about it?" Misha let the door slam and followed him into the living room. In awe, she listened to him go on about the message they wanted to send with the piece. "Did you come here to tell me how to do my job, Talib?"

He didn't answer straightaway. Instead, he strolled the apartment, loving the soft warmth radiating from the comfortable yet elegant décor. He didn't comment, knowing she wasn't ready to hear compliments from him.

"I spoke with Gloria." He unbuttoned the hunter-green suit coat and eased one hip onto the edge of the dining table. "She agrees that a detailed human-interest piece is best. We'd like to show folks that Hud-Mason is more than another shallow company scraping up millions for pampered athletes." He folded his arms and stared thoughtfully at the artwork lining her walls. "We were thinking of maybe a three- or four-part series."

"Are you insane?" She bolted toward him. "I don't have time to devote to something *that* expansive! Talib!" She followed him when he left the table and disappeared down the hall leading to her bedrooms.

"Gloria gave it the green light and we don't want anyone else on it but you."

Misha was seconds away from raining blows across his back but she wouldn't give him the satisfaction of watching her come undone. "Would you just go?" She spoke as softly as she could.

"But we haven't had our breakfast yet." He was studying her DVD collection next to the flat-screen television in her master bedroom.

"I think you just explained everything we were going to discuss."

"And now we can enjoy our food without business interrupting."

She massaged the bridge of her nose and turned away when he advanced. "Business is the only thing between us." She sighed.

"Is it?"

Misha knew he was but a touch away without needing to look back and prove it to herself.

"Is it, Misha?" The back of his hand trailed the dip of her spine. His finger curled into the belt around her robe in case she had any thoughts of moving away.

"Is it?" he insisted.

"Talib, what do you want from me?" She almost moaned and received her answer seconds later.

She was turned promptly and kissed thoroughly. Like before, like always, she responded in kind. Her tongue thrust eagerly against his, giving as much fire as his gave. She was so intent on the kiss, so absorbed in that fantastic cologne he wore that she hardly registered him hoisting her against his body and following her down to the bed.

Finding her nude beneath the robe, Talib took full advantage. Without a care for his tailored three-piece suit, he threw himself into the task of pleasuring both Misha and himself. Misha bit her lip and let herself go. She'd denied herself a man's touch for so long. To now be with the man whose touch she truly craved bordered on heavenly.

Talib kissed his way down her body, almost painfully aroused by the supple curves on her slender form. Her bottom was full and molded perfectly to his palms when he cupped them beneath her. Her breasts were small, firm, perfectly rounded mounds that beckoned his lips, teeth and tongue. And when he had his fill of tonguing her nipples into a frenzy, he ventured lower.

Misha tunneled her fingers into the silky dark curls covering his head. Gradually, she took stock of their position—more accurately *her* position. Half out of her robe and flat on her back beneath a provocative, impeccably dressed male. Silently, she completed the admission which had been interrupted when Talib first rang the bell. The thought drained her arousal and instead of gripping his shoulders to draw him close, she began to push him away.

Talib tuned in easily and didn't try to coax her into going further. This wasn't the time, yet he was approaching the point where he nearly didn't care. This was happening far more quickly than he'd expected, but then didn't everything where he and Misha were concerned?

He allowed himself a moment to graze his nose across her belly and the faint dusting of curls above her womanhood. Then he muttered something about letting her get dressed and left her alone.

Red Sun at 8:50 a.m. was of course a madhouse. The Japanese-owned eatery was anything but the usual. The breakfast menu spanned the globe and easily appealed to an extensive array of tastes.

Misha couldn't find a thing she wanted to order. Talib handled it all as though her sour mood hadn't fazed him. She snapped her fingers suddenly as if she'd been wracking her brain to come up with a discussion topic and finally latched onto one.

"We should set up some meetings to cover the story."

"Later, all right?"

She was opening her mouth to insist.

"I also wanted to invite you to a party."

"With you?"

Talib stroked his jaw. "Isn't that the way it's done, love?"

"I can't, I... The baby, the baby's party put me so far behind." She fidgeted with a lock of her hair. "I just don't have the time."

"I haven't even told you when it is."

Misha clenched her fist beneath the table and waited.

"Consider it research for the story." Talib smiled as their waiter approached. "It's for a new client—about a week and a half from now."

Misha managed to remain silent until after her coffee and Talib's tea had been placed on the table.

"You really have lost your mind, haven't you?" She flopped back on the redwood chair and laughed shortly. "Either that or you're just in need of a little side entertainment while you're in town and torturing me is the best you could come up with."

"Maybe I *am* daft." Talib spoke as if he were talking to himself. "Because I've got absolutely no idea what you're talking about."

"Do you remember the last client party I attended?"

Talib frowned. "Vic?"

"Not Victor." She rolled her eyes then glanced across her shoulder to see if anyone had noticed her outburst. "Ray Simmons," she hissed.

Talib had truly forgotten, for his powerful frame tightened visibly the moment he heard the name. He was quiet, coolly going about sweetening the hot tea in the mug before him.

Misha was about to take a sip from her black coffee when Talib's fist suddenly came down on the table.

"Will we ever get past all that?" He grimaced, not expecting an answer. "I guess not, especially when you won't even let me talk to you about it."

"*It* ruined us." Pain clearly colored her words. She kept her eyes focused on her coffee. "But it was only one of the things that ruined us—all the rest built slowly."

"Crickey, Misha, what *rest?*"

"Come off it. I was never good enough for you and you made that pretty damn clear when the Ray Simmons story broke. How many times did you say my supposed betrayal was something you should have expected from a woman like me? A slut that would sleep with a man for a story? And why not? Hell, I grew up with nothing, so why not do whatever it takes to have it all, right?"

Talib was speechless and stunned. He watched her as though suddenly realizing what her anger, her fear, was about.

Misha looked away, stunned as well that she'd admitted so much. She kept her face turned when the waiter arrived with their meal.

"Misha..." He didn't know what else to say when they were alone.

She considered it a blessing when they were interrupted again seconds later by a few men who'd gotten wind of Talib's presence at the restaurant. Of course they all recognized Misha, admiring her blatantly as they greeted.

"Why don't you guys stay?" She left her chair quickly, waving at the fruit, croissants and cheese on her plate. "And help yourselves—this hasn't been touched."

She was almost home free when Talib caught her wrist on her way past him.

"We'll talk later, all right?" His thumb slipped beneath the cuff of her blouse to caress her bare skin.

"Not about..." She glanced back toward the table where the others were already making themselves comfortable. "Not about what I said."

"Sure, but we'll talk later, all right?" he insisted.

She had no choice but to nod.

"Very impressive, Mr. Hudson," Misha raved when she saw Asher leaving the elevator.

At once Asher's light stare was less serious and more playful. "Well, hey!" He approached his wife's best friend with open arms and enveloped her in a tight hug.

"I hope I'm not interrupting. I just needed to see you for a second."

"Stop talking silly." Asher kissed her cheek, then moved back to frown into her face. "Is everything all right?"

The words weakened her resolve and Misha cursed her visible reaction. Asher took heed and ushered her someplace more private.

"Sorry," Misha sobbed when they were behind the closed doors of Asher's office. She curled up on a sofa in the corner. "Thanks." She took a deep sip of the black coffee he provided.

"Stop apologizing and tell me what the problem is."

"What's Talib up to?" she asked the moment he joined her on the sofa. "Why's he so hell-bent on us... being friends all of a sudden?"

Asher's smile was slow and knowing. "I think you know he wants more than a friendship."

She nodded. "So it's about sex," she said as though that possibility were easier to handle.

Asher's chuckling filled the room. "It's about love."

"He doesn't love me."

"Now look. I've been friends with Talib for a while now. And even though he keeps mum as far as the two of you are concerned, I swear that he does. And what's more I don't think he's ever stopped. But I've already said too much." He took the cup she'd drained. "Y'all need to talk and stop avoiding it because you're afraid of the past."

"I can't handle that. I don't have the strength—not a second time." She pushed her hair away from her face and cleared her throat. "He'll see that…he'll see once he's done deluding himself that two people like us never had a chance."

"Well, I can't speak to whether he's deluding himself, but I do know Talib Mason is a finisher. He doesn't quit midstream." Asher made a bridge with his fingers and shrugged. "This may not sit well with you, but I don't know what will make him stop until he's seen this through to the end."

Misha arrived late to the daily budget meeting for *The Stamper Court.* The business crew always gave their input toward the end of the meeting. Staff writer Trenda Greene was giving her report when Misha got there.

"You okay?" Riley asked when Misha took the seat next to hers and nodded quickly.

"Is there anything else, folks?" Riley addressed the group when Trenda concluded her report. "Wendell?"

"We all know this subject's taboo here at *The New Chronicle.*" Wendell Stevenson tapped a hand to the stack of papers he stood before. "But I feel it's important to note that our competition has seen healthy revenue increases since they've added entertainment sections to their pubs."

Everyone groaned. Some threw wadded balls of paper at *The Stamper Court*'s accountant. Overall, *The New Chronicle* family was pretty much in agreement that celebrity gossip wasn't the sort of news they were interested in. Since one of their own ran in such circles, much of that agreement was in a show of support for Riley's and Asher's right to privacy. Besides, Cache Media, the *Chronicle*'s parent company, never complained of the money woes which had driven the competition to incorporate more sensational news into their publications.

"I just think it deserves to be mentioned!" Wendell smiled when the group silenced. What the accountant lacked in height, he made up for in strength of voice. "The brass at those pubs are already crediting their entertainment inserts with the revenue surge—more revenue means more readers. Readers who most likely *aren't* reading our paper."

"Thanks, Wendell." Riley made a note to her agenda. "The *Court,* as you know, wouldn't be able to accommodate such a section, but you're welcome to carry your suggestion higher up the chain."

"Yeah, Wendell, maybe you could write the first piece." Frederick Mears's comment roused a chuckle from the table. "I've heard rumors of a boxer who may be havin' an affair with his sister."

"All right, everybody. Meeting adjourned! Thanks, Wendell." Riley smiled apologetically. She and Misha remained seated while the room cleared. "You look drained," Riley said while swiveling her chair to and fro.

"I just saw your husband."

"Ah." Riley folded her arms across the gold cap-sleeved sweater she wore. "He *does* have that effect on women." She tilted her head, hoping to rouse a smile from Misha.

It worked, but only for a moment. "He said Talib loved me—that he wouldn't give up until he saw this thing through between us."

"How do you feel about that?"

Misha only shook her head.

"You know whatever's happening or about to happen is only gonna put you through more hell unless you step up and face him."

"Humph." Misha rested her head against the chair and smiled. "You're right."

"'Course I'm right." Riley nudged Misha's boot with the tip of her pump and believed she was seeing the first genuine smile her friend had produced in days. "Why are you giving him all this control over your emotions, anyway? Show him who you are, who you've become. Make him eat his words for requesting you on this story. Torture him a bit. The driver's seat should be shared, right?"

Misha shook her head over Riley's cunning. "You've definitely been hanging around me way too long."

Chapter 4

Talib was tapping an envelope to the crease of his trousers when Asher walked into the office the next morning. Finding his partner perched on the edge of the desk and staring past the windows brought a slight sharpness to Asher's expression. Then he noticed Talib scan the envelope and smiled.

"That what I think it is?"

"An invite to Jasper and Molly Faison's couples' weekend," Talib explained.

"When they first mentioned it last year, I was sure it was just talk." Asher grinned and went to shuffle through the folders his partner left for him to review. "Why'd *you* get an invite?"

Talib laughed shortly. "No bloody idea."

"So whose day are you gonna make by asking?"

Talib studied the invite again. "There's only one *who* that I'd want to take."

"Misha." Asher settled down in an armchair before the desk and crossed his legs at the ankle. "You know there's a good chance she got one of those, too."

A low sound rumbled in Talib's throat and he tossed the dainty envelope to the desk. "Do you think she'd take someone else?" He looked around to see Asher shrug. "You know something." He turned to face his friend. "Is she seeing someone?"

"Calm down, Tal." Asher easily recognized the rising rage in his partner's dark eyes.

"Has Riley said anything?" Talib left the desk and walked over to observe the cloudy day. "Hell, it'd make sense if Misha was seeing someone. She's…an incredible woman. And I've certainly got no claim to her."

"Would you stop this, man?" Asher grimaced and walked over to slap Talib's shoulder. "Why don't you just ask her to go? See what she says."

Talib stroked his jaw methodically, turning the idea over in his head.

"You're afraid she'll say no if you ask?"

"Half." He leaned on the window. "The other half is afraid she'll say yes."

Again, Asher slapped Talib's shoulder and turned for the office door. "I guess you just have to ask which half you're more afraid of."

Misha was seated at a table in the popular but unusually quiet Orton's Café. To her delight, she'd beaten the lunch crowd and secured a cozy table with a fine view of the rainy conditions past the bay windows lining the establishment.

Unfortunately, the view was lost on Misha as she was currently engaged in an agitating phone conversation with her best friend.

"Well, I had nothing to do with it," Riley insisted. "And you knew Jas and Molly were planning it when we were all out at Vic's ranch."

Misha slumped against the booth as her memory freshened.

"And they probably just invited everyone who was out there. Anyway..."

"Anyway...?" Misha prompted as she straightened. "Riley?"

"I mean it's...it's understandable that Molly would invite you and probably Talib, too. Anybody can tell there's still emotion there."

"Well, I haven't—"

"Now hold on, just hold it." Riley's voice was near a whisper. "I don't even think you or Talib are aware of what you give off. In my very humble opinion, I say you guys should at least talk it over, lay all your cards on the table. Maybe that's all it'd take to start moving past all the drama."

"Easy for you to say." Misha rolled her eyes at her laptop resting on the table.

"Hey, I've been there, remember?"

"I remember."

"So let me share what I've learned, okay? Maybe you

can get some use out of it. Heck, put it to use tonight at Vic's dinner party."

"Crap."

"You forgot about that, didn't you?"

Very much so, Misha silently confessed to herself. *The New Chronicle* had put together a celebration to honor its former employee and his first year as a professional basketball player.

"Thanks for reminding me."

"Where are you, anyway? What's all that background talking?"

"I'm gonna try to help Coyt fine-tune his revisions to some of his pieces."

Riley laughed. "Good luck with that."

Misha nodded, thinking of their overly descriptive junior staff writer. "Anyway, we're meeting over here at Orton's."

"Well, I'll let you get to it, then. Think about what I said, all right?"

Misha promised to do so and was tucking the cell into her bag when she looked toward the café's entrance for Coyt. She found Talib Mason entering instead, along with two men she didn't recognize.

"More hot water for your tea, ma'am?"

Misha looked away quickly from the front of the restaurant and barely nodded to the waiter's offer. She thought about the invite tucked away inside her purse and wondered if Talib had gotten one. He probably had a string of women to choose from as his date. She tried to deny the stab of jealousy the thought evoked.

Risking another glance, she saw Talib and his group had moved on. Just as well. Sighing, she turned to her laptop and focused on one of Coyt's pieces.

Talib settled for hot tea while his companions asked for black coffees.

"We think Duck's a phenomenal guy—phenomenal stamina, phenomenal intelligence—simply phenomenal."

The more "phenomenal" Ducker Conrad sounded, the more certain Talib became that Wade Casey was at his wit's end.

"He's giving you trouble, I assume?"

The vice president of the Nevada Blaze appeared to lose some of the stiffness in his shoulders. "We'd like to keep this quiet, Talib. No need for Duck to get wind and get bent out of shape."

"More than he already is?" Talib asked.

Benny Austins chuckled. "You got a way with the kid, Tal. Everybody knows that. It could go a long way if you step in here."

"What problems are you having with him exactly?" Talib asked the Blaze's general manager.

Benny exchanged a frustrated glance with Wade and raised his shoulders slowly. "The kid just flips, Tal. Breaks bad over the simplest instruction. The coaches are almost fed up. You know how that kind of unrest can affect the rest of the players. And in that case there's only one solution."

Talib's grimace remained in place when the waitress

returned with their hot tea and coffee. It could be an agent's nightmare working to place an athlete once word spread of attitude trouble. The situation could turn into a nightmare regardless of talent or the reasons behind the unrest.

Wade Casey leaned forward. "Don't get us wrong, Talib. We want to keep Ducker with the team. He's got the skill and smarts to be one of the greats—all the coaches think so."

"If you and Ash could try talkin' to him," Benny urged, while lacing his coffee with an obscene amount of sugar.

"Maybe the fact that you guys are aware of what's going on might help him get on the good foot," Wade added.

"We'll try." Talib knew the promise was empty. It'd take more than he and Asher simply being *aware* of the trouble to do the trick with Ducker Conrad.

The waitress returned then for orders, but no one had even glanced toward the oversize menus on the table. The men focused on deciding their lunch meal and quiet settled all around.

Not surprisingly, Talib's attention returned to Misha. He'd spotted her three seconds after he'd cleared the café's front door. His conversation with Asher replayed silently. It hadn't veered far from his thoughts since that morning.

The possibility of her seeing someone was one he'd refused to entertain during the past six years. Dwelling on that particular possibility was dangerous and pointless to boot. And now? Now, it was just as dangerous but worthy of acknowledging.

And what then? Would he bulldoze his way over any other who thought to put up a fight for her? Would he back away and let her stroll off into happily-ever-after with someone else? While he wouldn't consider himself as coarse as to follow through with bulldozing over some unsuspecting soul, walking away wasn't an option. Walking away didn't even merit contemplation.

Moments later, though, Talib was revisiting his decision not to bulldoze some unsuspecting soul. He watched one stroll right up to Misha's table and take a seat.

The lunch meeting with the Nevada Blaze execs ended a little over half an hour later. Talib waited at least fifteen minutes past that. He was glad the café didn't serve alcohol until after 5:00 p.m. or he'd have downed at least six stiff drinks while watching Misha across the dining room with her date.

Instinct told him it was all probably work-related. More than once he saw them referring to her laptop. Sadly, common sense rarely prevailed during moments like this. Talib commended himself on at least having enough sense to wait until the poor sap left the restaurant. He left the waitress a hefty tip and headed toward Misha who was packing up to make her exit.

"Good afternoon."

She prayed he hadn't noticed her jump at the sound of his voice. Having already figured he'd not pay a visit to her table, she'd let her guard down. "Afternoon," she managed.

He scanned the booth. "Am I interrupting?"

"I'm just finishing up."

"May I have a minute?" He was already sliding into the seat across from her. "Will I see you tonight at Vic's party?"

"Well." Misha cleared her throat as if that would ease the pressure of her heart slamming hard and fast against her rib cage. "Since the *Chronicle*'s hosting the thing…"

"Mmm-hmm." Talib studied her hands, one rubbing inside the other. "And will I see you at Jasper and Molly Faison's couples' thing?"

"Why'd they invite you?" Misha blurted out, even as her eyes closed in regret over the question. "I mean, you, um…you were invited, too?" She attempted to save face.

"I was just as surprised. It's not like they know I'm seeing anyone."

"Are you?"

"Not at the moment." He pretended not to hear the interest shading her voice. "Not for a very long moment, actually."

Misha didn't bother hiding an expression which clearly stated she didn't believe him.

"And what about you?" He focused again on his hands as he inquired. "Seeing anyone?"

"Not at the moment," she sweetly countered.

"Ah, I see…not at this *very* moment."

Misha leaned back against the booth and produced a knowing smile. "He's a coworker. One of the writers for Riley's section."

"Did I ask?"

"In your way."

"So I guess you won't be taking him to Jasper and Molly's?"

Heart slammed ribs again. "I may not be *taking* myself," she muttered.

Talib rubbed his thumb along the table's silver edging. "I hear they've got a great palace out on Long Island—it would be a shame to deprive yourself."

"What do you want, Talib?"

"Go with me."

For a time, she could only stare. "Why? So we can be at each other's throats the entire time?"

Talib continued to study the silver grooves lining the table. "There's more than one way to be at each other's throats."

"Oh, Talib." Misha laughed. "What you want, you could get from anyone. Easily." She let him see the appraisal in her eyes.

Before he could take note of it, there was a rush of women to the table, all wanting an autograph from the former footballer. Obliging to a fault, Talib smiled and agreed.

Misha went about packing her things and checking dates on her calendar while Talib handled the adoring women.

"Pray tell why you wouldn't want to take a sure

thing on a trip like this." Misha slid a gaze toward the women who'd gotten their autographs and were moving on. Frequently, they cast looks back toward Talib.

"We need to talk," he said.

"It still comes back to that, huh?" She knew he was referring to her breakfast outburst days earlier. "It's still not something I want to discuss."

"You can't keep walking around it, love."

"There's no point in doing otherwise."

"Misha—"

"All right, look, I'll agree to go with you to this couples' thing on the condition that we drop this. We don't discuss it, period, take it or leave it."

Spreading his hands, Talib accepted the terms with a smile. He rose as smoothly as he'd taken his seat, kissed Misha's cheek and left.

Chapter 5

The New Chronicle put together an intimate affair for their former fact-checker Victor Lyne. That is, if one considered a guest list of one hundred *intimate*. Nevertheless, the event was a fun-filled affair with former coworkers of the talented forward. There was much laughter and reminiscing that evening. The fact that Vic had had a stellar rookie season made the night that much more enjoyable.

"Talib?" Misha waved while stepping closer to the man next to her. "Coyt Parsons," she said when Talib approached. "Coyt's a writer for *The Stamper Court*."

Talib's midnight stare reflected recognition. He offered Misha a quick smirk before shaking hands with Coyt.

"I was wrong for putting you through twenty questions

earlier," he said once Coyt had moved on through the party, "but any man would be out of his mind not to have entertained the thought."

"Exactly how do your female employees feel about harassment, Mr. Mason?"

"Unseemly advances from me are things they'd never have to worry about," he said as he brushed the back of his hand across her jaw. "You, on the other hand…"

"I, um…" Her gaze wavered and then brightened. "I need to go talk to Riley…about…something. Excuse me."

"What time shall I drop by on Thursday?" he asked as he blocked her exit.

"Talib, we can't—"

"We should probably hit the road early."

"This is stupid. We don't need to go to this thing together."

"Eight? Nine?"

Misha briefly hid her face in her hands.

"Are you afraid of me now, love?"

"Not a bit," she snapped back and dismissed the seductive allure in his tone. "You can pick me up at eight."

Talib's dimples flashed when Misha brushed past him.

Later, Riley and Misha lounged with their shoes off and their feet propped on the railing surrounding the balcony overlooking the city from Board Chairman Oliver Pacley's uptown penthouse.

"So who's gonna watch the little guy while you're at Jasper and Molly's?"

"I think it's my mom's turn."

Misha smiled, thinking of Virginia Stamper. "Must be nice to have babysitters vying for turns with the baby."

"Yes...*grandparent* is a beautiful word."

A sly smile curved Riley's mouth. "Ms. Frankie'll be lucky when the time comes." She referred to Misha's mother, Francheska Bales. "She'll have no other grandparents to compete with, unless Talib's family—"

"Hold it, Riley. Just hold it." Misha straightened in the wrought-iron chair she occupied. "We are *not* in that lane. Far from it and we probably always will be."

"So you're saying you wouldn't like to have his child?"

"Riley." Misha wilted. "Please stop."

"Honey, the two of you are gonna see a lot of each other while he's in town, you know? How are you gonna handle that?"

"I'll just have to do whatever it takes this weekend."

Riley's mouth fell open as Misha basically told her that she and Talib were going to the event together. "You know it's a *couples'* weekend, right, Meesh?"

"And we both got invites, meaning we'll both have our *own* rooms to share with our *own* date." Misha studied the button cuff of her blouse.

"And how much time do you expect he'll let you spend away from him?"

"Wasn't it you who told me not to let him keep taking the upper hand? And you were right. I've got to make the effort. Otherwise I'll wind up some simpering idiot every time I see him."

Riley reached over and squeezed Misha's foot. "Funny how love does that to a woman."

Misha winced, recalling the time she'd once said something similar to her friend.

Chapter 6

"Hungry?" Talib asked as he pulled into the side street convenience store/café.

"I'm fine," Misha insisted.

"Don't you at least want a sandwich or something?"

"Talib, we should really get a move on. With all this stopping we won't get there until nightfall."

"Does that make you nervous? Being on the road with me after dark?"

Misha rolled her eyes. "Don't be stupid."

Talib parked and shut off the car. "Do I make you nervous?"

"Now *that* really *is* stupid."

"Is it?"

"Do you want me to be nervous?"

"I want you to be many things. Nervous is definitely not one of them."

Misha rolled her eyes and was about to look away when he captured her chin and followed the action with a slow, thorough kiss. Misha sank into it before it even registered that she was kissing him and wanting more, wanting so much more than a kiss.

Talib rose with the cooler head though and pulled away. "Come on. We've got time for a quick bite. I promise to have you safe and sound at Jasper and Molly's by nightfall."

Misha watched him leave the truck and head around to open her door. All the while, she prayed her legs would work. Luckily they did, and soon they were seated at a small table inside the café.

"I hope this isn't some excuse to talk about what I asked you not to mention."

"The only one *mentioning* that right now is you." Talib studied his menu but set it aside as a thought occurred. "Have we ever discussed the consequences of breaching the forbidden subject?"

"What do you expect to come from this?"

He reached for the menu again. "An easy lunch, light conversation," he said smugly.

"I mean what do you expect to come from this attempt at being civil?"

He leaned back against the booth. "I was a jerk, Misha, and if civility between us is all that comes from me finally acting like I've got a brain in my head, so be it." Once again he picked up the menu. "Now what are you ordering?"

* * *

Jasper and Molly Faison's Long Island retreat was the perfect setting for what was in store for the weekend. With an exquisite view of the Long Island Sound from the rear of the house, the lawn was set with cushioned chairs and umbrella-covered tables. A self-serve bar sat in their midst, fully stocked and ready to appease even the most diverse tastes.

Inside, the surroundings were just as mellow, just as provocative. Soft lighting glowed throughout and smooth music piped into every room. As the couple traveled constantly, they each knew the value of sharing time, hence the retreats they loved to have with their friends.

Billiards and dancing were the order of the evening. Misha, who took pride in her skills, felt far safer at a pool table than on the dance floor, as her partner would of course be Talib Mason. The atmosphere was heavy with seduction as practically every couple huddled, cuddled or snuggled across the expanse of the glass-encased den/rec room.

"I know how to play the game, Talib." Misha's lashes fluttered as he moved in closer to assist with her hold on the cue.

"Not as well as I do."

She turned with challenge in her eyes. "What are you willing to bet I can take you?"

He smiled down dangerously. "We don't need to place a bet for you to take me, love."

Misha smiled, but inched away just the same.

"We lucked out with those adjoining rooms, eh?"

"Right. Luck." Misha glared toward Riley who twirled on the dance floor with Asher. She wondered how much of the room arrangement was coincidence and how much had been orchestrated by her crafty friend.

"So about this bet," Talib said as he sharpened his cue, "if I win you sleep in my room, if you win I sleep in yours."

"And exactly who comes out the winner there?" Misha laughed. Seconds later, her stomach lurched at the sinful change of Talib's features.

The evening's events lasted into the early-morning hours. Guests trickled off to their suites in other areas of the house. Meanwhile, the piped-in music transitioned from up-tempo to slow and sultry, befitting the various private events taking place throughout the dwelling.

Misha and Talib ventured to their adjoining suites, and it appeared that no private events were going to be taking place between them that night.

After regretting this for the entire night, Talib decided to remedy the situation the next morning. Around eight-thirty he was rapping on the door adjoining his and Misha's suites. She eventually answered—drowsy, disheveled and quite agitated.

The smell of coffee wafting beneath her nose was an effective wake-up call. Talib held the mug just out of her reach, gesturing for her to cross over into his suite.

Craving the coffee, Misha didn't argue. Seconds later, she was seated cross-legged in the middle of his bed and enjoying the black, flavorful brew. "What are you doing up while everyone else is still dead to the world?" she asked.

"Half the house was otherwise engaged for the better part of the night and morning." He appeared crestfallen. "I didn't have that problem, unfortunately."

Understanding then what her wake-up call was for, Misha set the mug down. But her intention to leave the bed was foiled as Talib sat down beside her and captured her lips in a deep kiss. She was in his bed and he intended to keep her there.

Her body had every desire, except to resist.

Talib kept her there for what seemed to be a never-ending session of irresistible foreplay. The cami and shorts she'd worn to bed were in total disarray as his fingers plundered beneath them and his mouth devoured hers hungrily.

Misha groaned her disappointment when his fingers withdrew from the part of her that ached shamefully for him. But she quickly forgot it when she felt his mouth there. Hooking strong hands around her thighs, Talib kept her still while he feasted.

"Talib…wait…" She wanted him to pleasure her, of course, but she wasn't ready to return the favor in the way she knew he needed. "It's not fair…" she moaned, riding his tongue slowly "…not fair to you…"

Not wanting to do anything against her wishes, Talib stopped. Misha wouldn't risk eye contact when he finally let her up. Just barely, she made it to the adjoining door. Her weakened legs finally gave out just as she returned to her own bed.

* * *

A wine-and-cheese gathering was held that evening at sunset. The faint chill of the approaching autumn didn't overshadow the enjoyable event.

Misha saw Talib and Asher talking near the bar and braced herself as she walked over. Asher caught sight of her first and broke conversation with his partner to draw her into a hug.

"Sorry to interrupt you guys." She smiled when Asher kissed her cheek. "Could I, um, have a moment?" She looked at Talib.

"Catch you later, man." Asher clapped Talib's arm and gave Misha a squeeze before leaving the couple alone.

"We can't do this," she blurted, albeit softly.

Talib appeared confused. "Talk?"

She rolled her eyes. "You know."

"Remind me."

Balling her fists, she knocked them against the sides of her lavender trousers. "This will only put us in a bad spot while we're trying to work on this story."

Talib was clearly having a good time feigning bewilderment. His sleek ebony brows drew near above his dark eyes. *"This?"* he queried, while stoking his jaw.

"This morning in your room—" her stare faltered "—in your bed."

"Did you enjoy that?"

She could have swooned right there at the bass lining

his accent. "That's not the point. Sex was never our issue."

"I seem to recall us making an *issue* of it many times."

Misha felt her cheeks burn and knew her complexion was betraying her. "It was never a problem, but it could be if we mix it with trying to work on this feature."

"Right." He appeared to be considering the matter. "But what about using it to work on us?"

Misha stared at his mouth, certain she'd heard him wrong. Then someone called his name and he left her to dwell on the question.

Board games, debates, cycling and barbecues filtered throughout the remainder of the weekend. All the activity was a welcome diversion for Misha, who'd found herself reeling from Talib's suggestion that they work on themselves. He couldn't really be hinting at some sort of reconciliation, could he?

She shook off the thought and looked toward the dining-room entrance where the group was meeting for the final dinner of the busy weekend. Talib stood there talking with their hosts Jasper and Molly Faison.

A voice surged through Misha's muddled thoughts, asking if reconciliation was so out of the question. After all, wasn't it what she hoped for? Wasn't it what she'd only admit to herself in the quiet loneliness of her home?

Bowing her head then, Misha sat pressing her fingers to the bridge of her nose when Talib walked past her chair. He brushed the back of his hand between her shoulder blades bared by the V-cut of her dress.

"What time are we heading out tomorrow?" she asked once he'd taken his place next to her at the long, elegantly set table.

"Are you in a hurry?"

She propped her elbow on the table and shrugged. "All of us can't own multibillion dollar sports agencies, now can we?"

Talib shrugged then, too. "Jasper and Molly said a few people might make a longer weekend of it—stay through Monday or Tuesday."

"No, Talib." Misha blinked and glanced around to see if anyone had overheard her.

He rested against the highbacked oak chair. "Does spending more time together make you uneasy?"

"Cut it out." Misha gripped the side of her chair when she turned to fully face him. "Stop acting like you have no idea what you're doing."

"What am I doing, love?"

"You know damn well, so stop wasting your time. We're not going back there." Her anger then abated to something more melancholy. "We can't *ever* go back there."

Talib squeezed her thigh to keep her from turning on the chair. "I don't want to go back there, either. *There* was hell and I never desire to go back. But, we did leave things unfinished there."

"Talib—"

"And they need to be handled one way or another."

"Why?"

His smile returned then, purely seductive and full of promise. Satisfied that he'd properly unsettled her, Talib turned to the tables. "By the way, the party's next Wednesday night at seven. The boxer we're signing."

"You were serious about that?"

"Of course, why not?"

Misha looked away, not able to read the message lurking in his bottomless gaze. She thought of Riley's advice to stop letting him take the upper hand, to stop letting him turn her mind to mush, and damned if he wasn't good at that.

She was sick of it and knew it couldn't hurt to turn the tables a bit. Talib, however, had mastered a game she wasn't quite familiar with. So it all came down to one question. Would she be in way over her head if she tried to play along?

Chapter 7

"Misha?"

Talib's hushed tone made her laugh and made her decision to take things into her own hands well worth the effort.

Talib most likely didn't agree with that, as he was currently studying her with a mix of surprise, awe and embarrassment. The embarrassment most likely stemmed from the fact that he was dripping wet and barely holding his robe together when he answered the door.

"What are you—"

"Have you forgotten already? I'm picking us up for our date. In spite of my record, I thought I'd drive."

Talib's lashes fluttered. "I wish you'd stop saying that."

Misha rested against the doorjamb. "Are you going to invite me in?"

"Sorry." He instantly recalled his manners and backed away from the door. "I just got out of the shower."

Misha allowed herself a long, leisurely appraisal of his glistening, honey-toned frame. She tilted her head and studied the area where he held the robe loosely at his waist. She smiled, making eye contact again. "That's very obvious."

Momentarily taken aback by her demeanor, Talib paused. He shook his head after a second and waved her inside.

"It won't take me long to get ready. It's still early."

"No problem." Misha followed him into the hotel suite. She wasn't quite ready to stop admiring the stunning breadth of his back and shoulders and the long, powerful bare legs beneath his robe.

Talib was motioning toward the living area. "There's info on the guy we're having the party for if you wanna know more."

Misha paused in the process of removing her wrap. "You're really serious about involving me in this, aren't you?"

"Quite." He threw her a wink before heading into the bedroom.

She tossed aside the black wrap covering her dress and took a peek inside the portfolio. She took note of the name: Sampson "The Stone" Hart. The face was a good one—too good to risk in a boxing ring, she thought.

There was a thud, followed by a curse a few seconds later.

"You okay?" Dropping the portfolio, Misha strolled to the back and was lucky enough to catch another glimpse of Talib's physique. Her luck was better this time around for she got to observe the man without his robe. Her view was aided by the floor-length mirror on the closet door, but it was adequate enough for allowing her to study him without him knowing.

It pleased her to put more of a visual to all the hardness she'd felt against her during the couples' weekend in his bedroom. She could have watched him all night. The sinews in his back flexed impressively as he smoothed lotion into his skin. His wet hair covered his head in adorable blue-black ringlets. She smiled, watching as he went to search his suitcase. He hobbled a bit, favoring his foot which he may have stubbed earlier and accounted for the dull thud and curse she heard, Misha thought.

He bit his lip while concentrating on matching socks with the boxer shorts he'd chosen. Her breath caught when he finally turned, giving her the full benefit of his nude body. Yes, all of what she felt that morning was definitely him.

"Be out in a sec!"

His voice jerked Misha back to her senses. Quietly, she hurried back to the front of the suite.

Favreau's Bar was the site of the party for middleweight contender Sampson "The Stone" Hart. The bar was the

perfect setting as its layout was a multilevel space with a bar in every corner. Guests were allowed to branch out and enjoy conversations all over the establishment and not have to wait long for their drink refills.

"As we're trading places this evening, shall I wait on you to open my door?" Talib asked when Misha pulled to a stop before the bar's entrance.

"If you'd like," she said as she smirked and turned to face him. "The men in there would be more in awe of you than they already are. Seated in the passenger seat while a beautiful woman—" her large dark eyes sparkled devilishly "—opens your door. Ha! They'd be impressed as hell."

She was about to leave her side of the Acura when he grabbed her hand.

"You wouldn't have to open my door to impress them."

Misha wouldn't allow his looks or his voice to hold her captive for long. She exited the car, took the valet ticket and met Talib on the other side of the car.

"This is a lot of fanciness, Mr. Mason. Favreau's regular patrons won't know what to think." She teased, staring up and around at the surroundings.

"We wanted a lot of hype surrounding Hart." Talib pressed a hand to Misha's back, urging her to precede him into the bar. "The guy's not very good with the media, or people in general, for that matter. We're hoping a series of parties might help."

"Good strategy," she commended when they stopped at the coat check area put in place especially for the event. "What?" she queried, turning to find Talib staring. She'd noticed the look on his face before they left the hotel, but didn't take time to question it.

Then, it dawned on her that it was the dress. At first she thought the frock was a bit over-the-top, but she went with it anyway. The wine-colored material fit like a glove, only flaring out at her knees and where the long sleeves hugged her wrists. The drawstring bodice cupped her breasts provocatively and gave her a playfully chic look. She took the arm he offered, silently commending her choice while they stepped into the bar.

The party was for "The Stone," but Talib and Asher garnered more than their share of attention. Asher was thrilled to see his partner. He and Riley had been working the crowd since arriving over a half hour earlier. The man was ready for a little dance time with his wife.

No matter, for Talib was fine with working the crowd—even if it was something that really wasn't his cup of tea. Having Misha on his arm changed that.

She sensed the possessiveness in his touch, but wasn't about to let it go to her head. Showing up at his hotel that night had given her a much-needed power boost, but not enough to give her a false sense of being something she wasn't. They still hadn't discussed what she'd blurted out that morning at Red Sun during breakfast.

She didn't have the time to mull over anything further. She was being introduced to everyone who called Talib's name. But before any business was discussed or any congratulations were given, Talib made sure the woman

on his arm was recognized. He barely let her out of his sight for a moment. He even seemed a bit put out when she insisted on some private time in the ladies' room.

"Well, you're sporting a lovely piece of arm jewelry tonight."

Misha was finishing with her lipstick when she heard the familiar voice. Laughing, she leaned over to hug Shawny Reed, publisher at *The First Beacon*.

"In fact, I think any woman here would trade every bit of her jewelry to wear that Talib Mason." Shawny ruffled the brunette waves rippling down her back.

Misha waved off the comment and checked the wrapped locks framing her face. "It's just business, Shawn."

"Trust me." Shawny turned from the mirror. "When a man like Talib Mason is involved, *business* is the last thing it is."

"So how are things going at the *Beacon?*" Misha asked, trying to change the subject. "I heard through the vine that you guys are enjoying an impressive revenue stream with your new entertainment section to thank."

Shawny rolled her eyes. "Yeah, everyone these days is more interested in what toothpaste a celebrity uses than in the state of world affairs."

"Well, Justine Duke must be doing a bang-up job." Misha studied the ruffled cuff of her sleeve and feigned light interest.

"I wonder how long it'll take for our readers to notice almost every piece has her byline."

"And why is that, anyway?" Misha asked as they strolled from the restroom corridor.

Shawny's green eyes narrowed. "*That* is because she's the top lady in charge—everyone else is just a lowly assistant."

"And you're letting her get away with it?" Misha halted her steps.

"Trust me, I'd love to kick the woman out on her talentless butt but the board loves the cash she's bringing in."

Misha winced, understanding the woman's predicament. "Well, let's just hope all good things will come to an end."

"You got that right." Shawny rolled her eyes and accepted Misha's hug before they parted ways.

Talib appeared quite relieved when he found Misha on the enclosed balcony overlooking the city.

"I've been looking all over for you." He rubbed her hair between his fingers when he passed.

"I'm just taking a minute."

"I'll take one with you."

"You can't." Her mouth fell open when he dropped down next to her on the loveseat nearest the balcony railing. "You've got all these people here wanting to talk to you."

"They'll survive while we have our minute."

"Talib?" Misha bit her lip, hesitating before she broke her own rule and decided to continue. "Is this about what I said at Red Sun—what I hoped we were done discussing?" She turned toward him on the seat. "Because I'm a big girl. I'm a big, successful girl who doesn't need anybody to welcome her into their club."

"Misha, do you really think you could tell me something like that and not expect me to do anything about it? Granted, the way things ended…it makes sense that you'd have that idea, but I have the feeling you felt this way long before all that craziness with the story…."

"It's in the past, Tali." She pressed her lips together following the slip.

He tilted his head to keep watch on her face. "Funny how all those things in the past are still screwing with us, eh?"

"We can't change anything."

"And I hate that," he muttered, seconds before his tongue thrust into her mouth.

Misha was moaning and thrusting back as the kiss heated and moistened. Like before—like always—need surged quickly between them. Talib had thought of getting inside the bodice of her dress since he'd first seen her in it. Now his hand was there, cupping a full mound, his thumb brushing her nipple as it firmed.

"Come home with me." He kissed his way down her neck. "Come home with me."

"Of course I will." She cupped his cheek. "I've got to drop you off."

Talib let his head rest on her shoulder as a wave of chuckles claimed him.

"Did you plan this?" he asked.

"I'm a working girl, remember? Gotta get home at a sensible hour. Speaking of which, what time should we meet tomorrow?"

She tugged at his jacket lapel and he knew she was serious. "How about ten?" he suggested.

"Make it nine. My office." She smoothed his lapel and winked. "You can bring *me* breakfast."

"You got it." He leaned in to seal it with another kiss.

Misha pulled away before things got too serious. "Let's go, Mr. Mason. You've got more mingling to do."

"Come inside with me." Talib extended his offer once again as Misha slowed to a stop beneath the canopied hotel entrance.

"Not a chance." She left the Acura idling and turned to face him. "You keep forgetting I've got a big day tomorrow, preparing for our first interview and all."

"You could prepare inside my suite."

"Right! I think we're discussing two separate things."

"We sure are! *I* don't need to prepare, after all."

"Talib, please." Misha was about to succumb to a fit of laughter. "Let me say good-night. Besides—" she granted him a saucy wink "—you don't want to ruin your mystique by begging, do you? All those folks hanging on your every word tonight would be *sooo* disappointed."

Her words were meant as a tease to ease the sexual

weight that hovered like an anvil between them, waiting to fall. Talib didn't find the humor in them.

"I don't give a damn about my mystique."

Misha noticed a jaw muscle dancing a wicked jig when he turned his head. "I'm not sleeping with you," she said.

"And you're so certain that you won't?"

"I'm *so* certain that I won't." She glared across the dashboard. "All this sudden…stuff between us is only due to being thrown together so much lately, nothing else."

Talib's hearty laughter resounded in the car's interior. "You actually believe that, don't you?"

"And you will, too, once you step back and admit what's really going on here. Now," she said, reaching across him to open his door, "out of my car."

He wouldn't allow her to straighten. Instead, he hooked two fingers into the bodice of her dress and kept her in place next to him. Whatever she thought to say when she opened her mouth was silenced when he kissed her hard and deep. Instantly, she became an eager participant, curving her hands about his neck and arching her breasts high on his chest. The caress he supplied to the bend of her knee and higher had her second-guessing her certainty that she'd not wind up in his bed. The kiss ended suddenly and Talib gave her a little jerk to bring her back to earth.

"You can think again if you believe I won't do what it takes to have you back in every way." Slyly he grinned and fixed the front of her dress. "See you in the morning."

Misha watched as he left the car coolly while she sat staring after him in aroused wonder.

Chapter 8

Deep in thought, Misha reclined in her office chair and propped her feet on the cherry wood surface of the desk. Absently, she stroked the scar behind her knee and was still doing so when Talib arrived.

He watched her from just inside the office. Gaze faltering, he asked himself if he was really up for going through with the charade for a story he couldn't have cared less about.

Before the breakfast at Red Sun, he'd have said no. He would rather have taken her somewhere, kept her there, loved her, *made* love to her until she believed in him again. That was before. Now he saw how deep it all went for her. Did she really believe he felt that way?

Talib grimaced, shifting his weight to the other loafer-clad foot. Why wouldn't she think that? Considering the way things ended between them…it was ugly and uglier still when they returned to each other's lives during Riley's and Asher's ups and downs.

She had every right to be wary of him. The story had taken on a different meaning for him now. She thought she wasn't good enough for him. He was set on showing her that she was everything to him. Her voice jerked him back to the present seconds later.

"I'm sorry, I must've zoned out." Misha had noticed him looming in her office doorway.

"You okay?" He pushed off the wall and strolled farther into the room. A slight frown marred the otherwise flawless face.

Focused on business, Misha left the desk with pad and recorder in hand.

"Pen," she hissed. Turning back to her desk she bumped smack against Talib.

"Are you okay?" he asked again, settling his hands to her hips that time.

"I was just talking with someone who was at the party last night." She smoothed a hand across the collar of her black silk blouse. "It seems that things got ugly with your fighter afterward."

Talib closed his eyes and nodded while everything fell into place. He'd received the call about the scuffle first thing that morning and was glad he'd insisted on leaving early. They'd have never gotten out of there if the drama had occurred before their exit.

"It's a real shame." Misha was tapping the recorder

against the mauve split skirt she wore. "He seemed like a nice guy—he and his sister."

Talib smiled. "But you're really okay?" He couldn't ignore the drained tinge in her dark eyes.

Misha gave a resigned nod. "I promise. All I need is my pen." Her voice was hushed and she didn't trust herself to make eye contact with him. "I thought we could discuss the way I'd like to organize the story." She spoke on the way to her desk and sent him a saucy look across her shoulder. "That is, if it meets with yours and Gloria's approval."

"I'm pretty sure anything you outlay will be fine with Gloria and me."

"Hmm." She cocked a brow and flipped a few pages on the pad. "I was thinking that your and Asher's *enthusiasts* would enjoy a bit more background on you both. So let's take your career in the pros, for instance. Was it always your plan to play? A kid with a dream? People love reading those stories."

"It was more a means to an end."

The comment sent Misha's head snapping up. Question was evident in her sparkling onyx stare. Before she could inquire further, the phone buzzed.

"Damn."

Misha bolted from the chair and smoothed her hands across the skirt again, much to Talib's delight.

"Woman knows I'm in a meeting," Misha grumbled, snatching the phone from its rest. "Yeah, Carla, what's the emergency?" she greeted her assistant. "What?"

Her frown deepened. "Carla…what? You *have* seen him before, you know," she whispered.

Carla had been away from her desk when Talib arrived. Like everyone else on the floor, she'd quickly caught wind of the man's presence.

"I'm as interested as anyone else, you know."

"We're trying to get started in here, Carla."

"Well, can I get him some coffee or…anything?"

"He's fine."

"Damn right, he is."

"I didn't mean it like that."

"Right, Misha."

"Now can I get back to work?"

Across the room, Talib was having the best time watching her handle the call—he was having the best time watching her, period. He reclined a bit more on the sofa and enjoyed the way she leaned across the desk. Her hair covered her face as always and he imagined himself gathering it into a fist and drawing it away from her face as he took her. The image was enough to rouse a groan and Talib cleared his throat hoping she'd not overheard it.

Misha did overhear the clearing throat, though. "You're a dead woman if you or anybody else interrupts me again," she hissed to Carla.

"So sorry." She rushed back to claim the pad and her seat. "What you said about football being a means to an end—could you elaborate on that?" She was perched on the edge of her chair and prayed he wouldn't clam up on her.

"My goal was to get into college." He focused on his hands, rubbing one over the other. "Football talent allowed me to get there, once I stopped confusing it with soccer, that is." He grinned.

"But wouldn't you have gotten there anyway? To college, I mean? After all…"

Talib's head tilted when he gave her the benefit of his gaze. "After all what?"

"Well…" Misha crossed her legs again and had no problem being blunt. "Your family's well-off. A college tuition shouldn't have been a hardship."

Talib's dimples flashed when he smiled. "You've got the story wrong, Misha. A college tuition wasn't even in my mother's hemisphere."

"But?" Misha was processing the information and quickly trying to obtain more. "What about the rest? You've got family in parliament for Pete's sake."

"I didn't meet them until much later."

Misha was silent for quite a while. Chewing on the cap of her pen, she realized how very little she knew about the man despite the three years they'd been together.

Talib was quiet then, too, considering exactly how much to tell her just then. The decision was irrelevant moments later when his phone rang. He winked and then sent an apologetic smile Misha's way.

"Hey, Claudette."

"Ah! Talib, thank God!" Claudette Silver's usually easy tone was anything but. Asher Hudson's executive assistant sounded as though she were in the middle of a three-alarm fire. "I've tried to get in touch with Asher and had to leave him a message. Now the *issue* I've got here is having a tantrum on the other phone line and on his way out here, I might add."

Talib glanced back at Misha who was making notes on her pad. "What's going on, Claudette? What's the issue?"

"Ducker Conrad is what's going on."

"Blimey." Talib rolled his eyes and listened while Claudette explained.

Misha set aside her pad and watched Talib handle the call. This time it was her turn to savor the view. The way he strolled the room—head bowed as he focused on the issue at hand, massaging his nose and smirking as though the news on the other end of the line was no surprise.

"It's all right, Claudette, you did fine," Talib soothed and the woman quieted. "How long before Duck arrives? Mmm-hmm…right…I'll take care of it."

"When?" Claudette's voice wavered nervously through the line.

"Soon. For the time being, Asher and I will have to hold a conference call with the idiot. We should be calling you back by the time the bloke walks through the door."

"Well…if that's the best you can do…"

"It is. Don't worry, all right? Talk to you soon."

Misha was at her desk by the time Talib ended the call. She made a passable pretense at straightening papers.

"We're going to have to cut this short, love. I'm sorry."

"It's fine." Misha kept her back toward him. "We can reschedule any—"

She wasn't given the chance to finish. Talib turned her into a kiss that Misha believed she'd been craving from the moment he walked into her office that morning. He took his time massaging his tongue against hers in the same leisurely style that his wide hands massaged her waist.

"I'll see you for dinner tonight," he said once he'd ended the kiss.

"You don't have to do that. We can always schedule something else—"

"But don't you want more of the story?" He used her curiosity against her.

Misha averted her gaze and nodded.

Satisfied, Talib kissed her temple. "See you at seven."

Chapter 9

Riley was relaxing in the living area of her office and reading copy for an upcoming *Stamper Court* article. A local baker was being sued for sexual harassment.

"'…who allegedly molested his female cooks while the cakes were baking, so to speak…' Ah, Coyt, give me a break." She groaned.

Ahmad, who lay resting against his mother's chest, let loose a long burp.

"I couldn't agree more. My man knows crap when he hears it." She nuzzled his head and the baby laughed.

It didn't take much more for Riley to set aside the proof copy. She was far more interested in pressing kisses to Ahmad's tiny palm and fingers.

Misha waited a moment or two before she knocked on the partially opened office door. "Can I interrupt you and your younger man?" she asked when Riley looked over.

"Sure. We can pick this up later, right, guy?" Riley said as she cuddled Ahmad and smiled. "That's the thing about younger men, time is irrelevant."

Misha paused to kiss her nephew's head on her way to take a seat.

Riley's brown eyes narrowed as she observed her friend more closely. "So how was your meeting with Talib?" she asked once Misha had dropped into one of the chairs flanking the sofa.

"Did you know his mother couldn't afford to send him to college?"

Riley frowned. "But he was drafted from college, right?"

"'College was out of my mother's hemisphere.' That's what he said during the interview."

"You sure?" Riley smirked when Misha raised her hands in response. "I wonder what that's about?"

Misha crossed her legs. "I was hoping you could tell me. Has Asher ever mentioned anything?"

Riley was already shaking her head. "He and Talib became friends in school. I wouldn't be surprised if Asher knew very little about his life before that, especially if it was troubled. People often go to college far away to meet new people, be part of a new world— forget the one they came from."

"Yeah," Misha recalled, having gone to college seeking the same thing.

Riley raised her chin. "What are you thinking?"

"I'm not sure." Misha leaned forward to rest her elbows on her knees. "I guess I just always had him pegged for some rich kid."

"Why? Because he's got a British accent?" Riley gave Ahmad a little bounce. "Trust me, girl, the U.K.'s got projects just like the U.S. does."

"I know, I know." Misha waved off the comment. "It's just a shock, that's all. We were together almost three years before… I never had a clue. Come to think of it, he never really talked about his mother or any of his family. I didn't pry because, well…it just wasn't who we were then. He only met my mother once." She slanted Riley a wink. "I didn't want to talk about my downtrodden life, either. It was time for upward mobility, success—the struggle was long passed."

"Long passed, but still a part of who you are." Riley thought how she'd tried to run from the troubles of her own youth by padding herself with work and goal-making. "I guess you're becoming intrigued by this feature article after all, huh?"

"I'm curious, only…"

"Only?"

"Dammit." Misha hissed and left the chair. "I just wish he'd stop touching me."

Riley laughed. "No you don't!"

Misha rolled her eyes. "Everyone doesn't become a swooning fool over a man the way you did when Asher Hudson appeared before *your* eyes."

Riley kissed Ahmad's head again. "Aunty's having trouble telling the truth."

"I can't focus on a single thing when he touches me." Misha smoothed her hands across her blouse sleeves. "I think he may be doing it on purpose to keep me off balance."

"And do you really mind so much? Really?"

"That time's over." Misha went to stare out the office windows.

"But the end for you guys came out of nowhere. Who knows how much of it has to do with the past he's now starting to share with you."

Misha's smile was tight. She'd been thinking that very thing.

A light but genuine smile tugged Talib's mouth when he stepped into the exotically furnished lobby of Misha's Manhattan building. He admired her cunning, knowing she was waiting there to avoid time alone with him in her apartment. He approached the security island slowly, taking enjoyment in her features which were even more lovely in the wake of laughter with the gentlemen she charmed.

The guards sobered, though, when they all spotted Talib.

Misha frowned, watching the men straighten and take stock of themselves. When she glanced around and realized their reaction was due to her "date" she only shook her head.

"I guess I don't have to make intros. Everyone already knows who you are," she said to Talib as he approached.

Talib was grinning and moving in to shake hands with the three guards.

"Congrats on branchin' out, Talib," Gary Carmichael was saying.

"Guess you ain't missin' the pros a bit, huh?" Gary's coworker Philip Shuster was asking.

Talib chuckled. "You kidding? Agents have the best of both worlds. We only have to get the players their paychecks—the rest is on them."

"Good luck to you, Talib." Sherman Benjamin shook hands and grinned as broadly as his colleagues.

Talib didn't bask in having his ego stroked much longer. Shortly, he was saying good-night to the guards and ushering Misha out to begin their evening.

"This is nice," he murmured, trailing his hands along the dress she wore. His dark eyes appraised the garment with its ruche bunching at the bodice. The rest was fitted black chic.

While she wouldn't swear to it, Misha had the distinct feeling that he'd been checking for the garment's fastening.

"Wow." Misha didn't mind letting her amazement show when she breathed the word. She'd visited the new building when she'd gone to see Asher. It had been the middle of the day then, though. There'd been no time for appreciating the spectacular view of the lit city beyond the towering windows.

She let her purse and wrap fall to a chair and strolled over for a closer look.

Talib followed but was more preoccupied by her dress than with the view. His hands glided across the material hugging her hips and bottom. Muscles flexed along his jaw and marred an otherwise cool expression when she inched away from his touch. He turned his back on the view and took a seat along the sill.

"So how much time will you get to spend in such a great office?"

Talib's laughter was brief. "Don't worry. It won't be much."

"Talib." She bowed her head to acknowledge the lack of subtlety in her question. "Can't you understand how…strange this is?" She raked her nails across the sleeves of the dress. "After six years of nothing and now…"

"And now I'm trying to make up for it." He smirked in spite of himself. "An idiotic move, maybe, but one I feel I have to make." He inhaled deeply and slightly averted his stare. "Am I too late, Misha? If I am, tell me." His throat constricted just as he managed to share the last of the statement. The last thing he wanted was her answer.

"What happens if this…whatever this is, works?" She gestured toward the view, hoping he hadn't noticed that she'd evaded his question. "We'd have another problem, wouldn't we? You won't be here, much."

Talib glanced across his shoulder then offered a flip shrug. "Compared to everything else going on between us, what's a few thousand miles?"

Soft laughter colored the quiet office.

* * *

Misha realized her earlier feelings were right on the mark, but acknowledged she could have still been misreading Talib's intentions when they arrived at his hotel a short time later.

"What are we doing here? Did you forget something?" She knew full well he hadn't.

Talib knew that, too. He granted her a wicked grin before leaving the Navigator and coming around to open her door.

Misha inched back from his hand. "Talib…"

"Dinner's getting cold, love."

Knowing it was useless to make an issue of it, she took the hand he offered.

Misha could have laughed over the turnaround had she not been so on edge. Just the day before, she was arriving at this room in this very hotel suave and in total control. Now she felt like a maiden being led to her deflowering. *Stop it, Misha!* The man simply wanted them someplace where they wouldn't be disturbed during the interview. It sounded plausible enough, so why didn't she believe it?

Talib certainly wasn't doing anything to help ease her concerns. The elevator ride hadn't seemed nearly so long before. This time, it positively dragged. Misha put distance between them in the car, which seemed pathetically tight when Talib made a point of invading her space. Misha opened her mouth to argue, knowing she'd never have the chance to speak.

She was right. Talib was kissing her seconds later. Had she known this was the plan, she'd have dressed far more conservatively. Talib's earlier inspection of her dress offered him expert reign over every inch of it.

"Talib, someone could—" She gave into another eager kiss before willing herself to pull back again. "Talib someone could get on—"

"I'll stop then, I promise."

The intensity of his caresses and the rapacious thrusting of his tongue offered Misha little hope that he'd keep that promise.

"Talib, please," she insisted when he held her high next to the paneled wall of the car. She couldn't believe that was her voice and she criticized herself for begging. She never begged. Men begged her—she *never* begged.

As she'd noted once, however, those men weren't Talib Mason. He hadn't a care for where they were, if the scandalous nature of his touch was any example. She was effectively pinned between the elevator paneling and the solid wall of his chest. His hands were free to cup and coax at will.

He found the lacy edge of her panties and she criticized herself again for wearing stockings instead of hose.

"Talib, mmm…" Then her high moan filled the car. Misha bit her lip in an effort to bring her breathing under control.

"This is my floor," Talib said and brought the pleasure-providing finger to his mouth and suckled off the moisture she'd planted there.

Misha barely recalled leaving the car.

* * *

"More?" Talib asked, glancing toward the strawberry shortcake he'd all but massacred.

Misha had nursed her first and only slice. Talib made her sit through a delicious yet lengthy meal. She found herself clearing her throat to mute the moans which plagued her infrequently as visions of their elevator romp replayed in her mind.

"Coffee?"

She waved away the offer and forced herself to regain a smidge of control over the situation.

"Are we going to discuss the story, Talib?"

"Of course we are." He wiped his hands and tossed the dark linen napkin to his dessert plate. "Where'd we leave off?"

Thankful, Misha grabbed her pad. "You were discussing college—its hardships." She reached for the pens that rolled across the table.

"Right." He grabbed a bottle and tipped it toward her. "More wine?"

Misha used both hands to wave off the offer. Instead, she grabbed back onto her pad and pens as though they were her lifeline.

"Why don't we move this into the living room?" Talib suggested, already standing from the table set next to the floor-to-ceiling windows overlooking the city.

Misha took the chair farthest away from the end of the sofa he'd chosen. Silently, she prayed he was still of a mind to be candid regarding parts of his past.

He was. Settling back, he took a sip of wine and considered his words.

"I wasn't a brain, but I understood the importance of school—the power it could afford. Seeing it through until the very end was my greatest goal."

"I'm sure that made your mother proud." Misha didn't look up from her pad.

"Yes. It would have."

Her pen stopped. She looked up in shock and was seconds away from her next question.

"Sit next to me."

She looked back toward her pad. "We should really make some headway with this."

"Which is my intention—don't you want to continue?"

"Yes." She scooted to the edge of her chair. "Yes, of course I want to continue." The curiosity was about to drive her insane.

"Sit next to me, then." He propped his index finger alongside his temple.

Curiosity won out over reluctance. Misha was planting her bottom to the sofa when he tugged her to straddle his lap. She melted into the kiss without argument…at first. Then, somehow, she drew back.

"You once accused me of sleeping with you for a story." Her fingers curved into the wintergreen shirt that hung outside his trousers. "Is that what this is?" He was kissing her throat slow and openmouthed and she was quickly losing her grasp on anything rational. "Talib?

Is this some trick?" She moaned. "I give in and in the morning you throw it back in my face?"

His mouth continued to roam her skin, then he cupped a hand around the base of her neck. "Quiet," he instructed.

She melted anew, not caring at all about what he threw in her face later. She wanted him and heaven help him if he thought to disappoint her then. She kissed him with an eagerness that drew what could only be surmised as a growl from his throat.

The scene had her throbbing and intent on claiming the orgasm she'd been desperately craving since he came back in her life. Boldly, she tugged at the fastening of his slate-gray trousers. She tugged more insistently, realizing he wasn't quite ready to give her access to what she sought.

Instead, Misha found herself on her back moments later and drowning in the pleasure of his perfect mouth on her body. When he finally let her up, she was limp, drunk on arousal and completely nude. He pulled her from the sofa and carried her to the bedroom.

Misha didn't care what she ripped while trying to get him out of his finely crafted shirt. She wanted to laugh once she tasted triumph. Her French tips grazed his honey-toned flesh, cut with an array of muscle.

They barely made it past the doorway. Tumbling to the floor, neither registered the contact as they kissed and caressed each other with smoldering, needy strokes.

Talib's mouth was everywhere, caressing, nibbling,

gnawing as he kept her on her stomach and worked his way down her body.

"Talib, please," she moaned. Desperate to face him, she knew he had no intentions of allowing that. Especially when he rose up behind, trapped her wrists before her and reached around to tease her nipples with his free hand.

Misha rested her forehead on the plush navy carpeting and submitted to whatever he had in store.

"Yes," she moaned when his finger drifted high between her legs and he sheltered one, two, three fingers inside the folds of her sex.

"Yes," she gasped in anticipation of release, then repeated the word as she rode his fingers.

She sobbed when he stopped short of her satisfaction. Anger ceased to sparkle in Misha's black stare when Talib put his hands on the buckle of his belt. Like a conditioned subject, she waited with her gaze riveted on the hands hovering at the belt. She didn't move, fearing he'd find some other way to make her wait.

Talib was done with that. He craved her as wildly as she did him. He wouldn't deny the arrogant surge rushing through him at the blatant lust and approval glittering in her eyes.

All fastenings undone, his trousers and boxers fell and Misha moved to her knees, not minding at all how sex-crazed she may have appeared.

"Give me a second, love," Talib urged as her lips and tongue traveled his torso. He was barely able to reach for the condoms in a cup on the nightstand.

He'd scarcely put protection in place before she was guiding him inside her. He winced, his beautiful features tightening in the wake of elation as her wet walls encased him. He noticed the slight frown mar her brow quickly and instinctively pulled back.

"Am I hurting you?"

Misha locked her legs around his back. "No. I'm okay."

He grunted something harsh and ragged, burying his face in the crook of her neck. He wanted her every way he could take her. Before the night ended, he damn well intended to accomplish that.

Just then, though, he only needed to be inside her. He needed her loving him, welcoming him, taking him.

Chapter 10

Misha woke, instantly expecting some ugliness in payback for her lack of control the night before. It had been beautiful, but so was every time between her and Talib. But that hadn't stopped things from souring, did it?

Squirming under the covers then, she could barely move. Talib was resting almost dead center across her body.

"Tali?" Her voice was soft because she was practically out of breath. "Tal?" She nudged her bottom against his shaft. She bit her lip, discovering that he was semi-hard even at rest. Someone give her strength.

"Talib?" Misha ordered more force to her voice then and gave him another nudge.

"Mmm?" He woke with a start, then settled back

down and favored her shoulder with a kiss. "You okay?" He curved an arm tighter about her waist.

Misha forgot any breathing discomforts then. The softness of his voice, his lips trailing her skin...this was no slap in the face and she wanted to enjoy it while it lasted.

Talib was waking though and turned her to her back to study her closely. "Are you really all right?"

Misha nodded, but failed to maintain contact with the dark eyes probing hers.

Talib understood, knowing she was probably mentally kicking herself because of what they'd done. Not much longer. Not much longer would she doubt them. He swore it.

"What would you like for breakfast?" He drew hair from her eyes and studied every inch of her face.

"Talib, I should go."

"After you eat."

"No. Now. It's bad enough to be leaving a hotel early morning in a cocktail dress. I won't make it worse by pushing my checkout time to noon."

"Well, I'm starved." He dropped a kiss to her nose. "And since I drove, you're stuck."

"That's what cabs are for."

Her flip remark was not well received. Once again, he smothered her with his weight.

"You once asked me to stop pretending I had no idea what I was doing. I'll ask the same of you now. Stop acting like you've got no idea what last night was about." His dark eyes seemed even more opaque as anger filtered his words. "Stop making it out to be some one-night stand."

"But wasn't it?" Misha swallowed her unease. "You'll be going back to Phoenix soon." She hadn't the nerve to question the sly dimpled grin he gave in response.

Her heart crept to her throat when he settled in snugly against her. Her moan wavered beyond parted lips when his hands roamed up under her back, forcing her breasts to flatten against his chest.

"It'd be best if you kept the majority of your responses to 'Whatever you say, Talib.'" He made the suggestion while nibbling her ear and collarbone.

She smirked. "Blindly follow you, in other words?"

He nuzzled the base of her throat. "I like the sound of that."

"What if I don't?"

"You will."

The kiss between them then merged into something Misha was certain would be an extension of the pleasure he'd reintroduced her to throughout the night and early-morning hours.

Talib was back to torturing her though. He broke the kiss while Misha was in the midst of driving her tongue hungrily against his.

"Get ready for breakfast," he said before slanting her a wink and leaving the bed.

"Sounds like this man still loves you."

Misha cast a frown toward the man seated cross-legged on the brown leather armchair. "Exactly how do men do that? Turn hate, love, desire, disgust off and on like a light switch? I've always been fascinated by that ability. Is it something learned or something you're all born with?"

Dr. Harold Zeitz gave a playful shrug. "Many times, it's a ploy to draw a woman in, lots of times they're terrified of her and trying to protect themselves, and—"

"Lots of times they really do hate and are disgusted by her."

Dr. Zeitz nodded. "But from what you've told me about Talib, if he truly hated or were disgusted by you then he'd not be going to such lengths to be with you."

"Unless he was formulating some plan to hurt me." Misha didn't care if she sounded paranoid. She glared at her therapist as though he should have at least suspected that possibility.

Dr. Zeitz uncrossed his legs and leaned back. "Do you really believe that?"

Misha shook her head no.

"Then what's the issue here? Why are you afraid to let this man in when it's obvious you love him, too?"

"How do you know it's obvious?" Misha whirled around, facing the doctor with amazement in her stare.

Harold Zeitz's handsome, tanned face softened more in the wake of humor. "Misha, I made a career of observing the things people say and do. You have no idea how your demeanor changes when you speak about Talib Mason." The doctor waved toward his patient.

"Today it's *very* obvious. This is the most you've ever spoken of him and even during those other times I've caught enough of a glimpse to clue me in to your feelings for him."

"Jeez," Misha groaned, flopping to the sofa and holding her head in her hands. "I've been doing just fine without him. The drama between us happened over six years ago. I've accepted that it's over. I'm successful. I've got lots of friends, some *very* good ones. I'm respected in my field and—"

"And without the man you love. Puts a bit of a shadow across all the rest, doesn't it?"

Misha appeared smug. "I can't think of one time I've felt depressed looking at my bank statement, Doc."

"Really?"

The simple inquiry broke through her steel shell quickly. She wilted. "He thinks I'm a slut. At least, he did the last time we were together."

"Did he say that?"

"He said 'only one type of woman sleeps with a man for professional gain' and that he should've expected it of a woman like me. So why don't *you* tell *me* what he meant."

"It sounds like he was hurting." The doctor trailed a thumb along the crease in his slacks and considered his explanation. "That hurt perhaps goes farther back than anything that happened between the two of you."

The doctor's words sent Misha deep into thought, as well. "His mother couldn't afford to send him to school.

I always assumed…she's passed away. I didn't know any of this until he told me for a story."

"Do you believe it's the only reason he shared it?" the doctor probed when Misha silenced.

"I, um…" She sat on the arm of the sofa and kept her back toward the therapist. "Some time before that, I blurted out that I was never good enough for him. I think I was just as surprised by the outburst as he was."

"Indeed. Especially with all your success and the great things you boast of."

"All right already, you've made your point." She pounded a fist to the sofa arm and stood. "I love him, so what? Love certainly didn't make things go so smoothly before."

"Perhaps that didn't have as much to do with you as you thought. Talib Mason sounds like a private man." The doctor traded the seat of his chair for the arm. "The road to getting him to reveal a deep-seeded issue may not be an easy one to travel."

"But necessary if I expect answers," Misha guessed.

"If you *want* answers."

"I do." She fiddled with a dangling earring and nodded. "I do. I've traveled hard roads before. Taking this one would definitely be worth it."

"And when you reach the end of it?" Dr. Zeitz turned his head toward Misha but didn't make full eye contact. "Will you be willing to turn the corner and share your own hurt?"

Misha couldn't answer that question.

* * *

Talib and Asher were laughing over a comment Claudette made about Ducker Conrad. Eventually, though, the conversation turned serious again as the three acknowledged they hadn't seen the last of the troubles surrounding their client.

Asher stroked the back of his hand across the scar along his cheek and whispered a curse. "This guy's got some real issues and I wish we'd taken more account of it before."

"He's a spoiled jackass is all." Claudette's voice sounded through the phone speaker. "We've dealt with these types before."

"Yeah, but sometimes, these *types* have to be handled a certain way," Talib added. "Many of those ways don't involve conference calls."

"Meaning one of you is gonna have to come back out here?"

Talib groaned. "One of us is gonna have to come out there."

Claudette was silent on the other end. The efficient assistant clearly assessed her bosses' need for a little privacy.

"It'll look better for you to be the one to go out and handle this, seeing as how the West will be your domain. Besides, you and Duck go way back."

Talib realized that it would have to be him long before he heard Asher speak the words. Nodding somberly, he stood and began to pace the office.

"Take her with you." Asher read his partner's mood again while leaning over to top off his coffee.

Talib laughed. "And by what means do you propose, my friend? Kidnapping or bribery? Surely you don't think my just asking would get the job done?"

Asher shrugged. "It might."

"Dammit, I need more time." Talib connected a fist to his palm. "I need a lot more time. Trust isn't an easy thing to win back, mate."

"Tell me about it." Asher grimaced. "So what about the story?"

Talib rubbed fingers through his hair and walked over to stare past the windows. "I've got her attention, but then I expected it. Before I started to…*share,* I never thought of how little she really knew about me."

"Man, she's a reporter and the woman who loves you. I'd say she's very interested in who you are." Asher chuckled then. "Hell, how long have *we* known each other? I don't even know the half of it, I bet."

Talib conceded his best friend's point with a nod. "My story isn't easily shared, but best forgotten."

Asher stood then and walked over to clap Talib's shoulder. "But you never truly forget, do you?"

Misha's frown was more confused than angry when she opened her door to Talib that night.

"I'm sorry." She tucked a wayward lock behind her ear. "We didn't discuss having a meeting tonight, did we?"

Shamefully long lashes settled slowly over his eyes

when he shook his head. "I took a chance you'd be home. There is something I wanted to talk to you about." His onyx eyes raked the length of her more than once. "Is this a bad time?"

"Um…well, I'm, um…entertaining."

Talib couldn't stop the sharp tug of his brows but managed to mask it easily. "Anyone I know?" He made a play at humor, hoping to restore his ease.

Misha shrugged. "Actually you know him quite well."

"Really?"

"I'm betting he'll be one of your clients someday."

"Is that a fact?" Talib eased a hand into the back pocket of his jeans.

Misha leaned against the door and rolled her eyes in a dreamy manner. "He's so young and full of energy, not to mention gorgeous. That's important, right?"

"Talent helps." Talib didn't mind if she heard the biting tone to the words.

Misha wasn't fazed. "Oh, I'm sure he'll have tons of that."

"Are you?"

"Definitely." She laughed then. "Would you like to say hello?"

Talib lingered in the doorway when Misha stepped back. "I shouldn't interrupt more than I already have."

"Oh, it's not a problem. He's just waking up."

Waking up? Talib smarted as if she'd slapped him.

"I'm just about to give him a bath." She left him in the doorway.

Frowning furiously then, Talib followed her into the apartment bent on satisfying his curiosity.

"Crickey, Misha," he whispered when she lifted Ahmad from the portable crib she kept for the baby's visits.

"Look who's here, cutie pie." Misha cooed to the baby and then fixed Talib with a saucy smile. "I think Uncle Tali was expecting someone else," she whispered near Ahmad's temple. "Exactly what *were* you thinking, Talib?"

He was already reaching for his nephew. "Just what you wanted me to."

"I'm babysitting." Misha propped her hands on her hips. "Asher and Riley had a last-minute thing."

Talib watched her close while bouncing Ahmad lightly against his chest. He took in her hair clipped up in a haphazard manner. Her feet were bare and peeking out from beneath the cuffs of her wrinkled black yoga pants and a strappy T-shirt splattered with what looked suspiciously like juice. Talib thought she'd never looked lovelier.

"May I help?" he asked when she realized he was staring.

"Sure." She headed out of the living room. "I'm always happy for an extra hand. It's not a big job, just a sponge bath. Looks like the guy's gonna spend the night."

The godparents worked in ease. Talib held conversation with the baby while Misha set out a pallet on her bed and ran water in a little wash basin from her private bathroom.

The baby laughed and was in constant motion, making it no easy task to rid him of his sleep clothes and diaper.

"So what did you want to discuss?" Misha wiped a damp, softly scented cloth across the baby's skin.

Talib waved fingers before Ahmad's face, smiling as the child followed every movement with an alert gaze. "It's good news, bad news or a mix of both depending on how one looks at it."

Misha maintained her duties but moved a tad slower as she waited for him to get to the point.

"There's an issue in Phoenix that needs a personal touch. It'll put our interviews on hold, I'm afraid."

"I see." Misha hoped she didn't sound as let down as she felt. It was hard to think of anything other than obtaining more insight into who the man was.

"But there may be a way to continue, you see…you could come with me."

Misha went completely still. "Your story isn't the only thing on my plate, you know? I can't just pick up like that."

She could and Talib knew it.

"Is this something you'd *insist* to Gloria?"

"Should I?"

"Could you at least let me think about it?"

"I can only give you a day."

"And how long would we be out there?"

Talib moved in to assist as Misha eased a one-piece tee over Ahmad's head.

"I don't really know how long, love. This problem is a real pain in the bum, which unfortunately requires my handling it personally."

"So it's about a West Coast client?" She watched him nod. "I suppose that makes sense."

"Meaning?" Talib cocked his head.

"Well, you'll be heading up the Phoenix office." Misha finished snapping the garment between the baby's legs. She gave Ahmad a little tickle then. "It makes sense for you to go out and handle a West Coast problem. It *is* still in the works for you to go back there, right?" Her tone was softer but nonetheless curious.

"It's still in the works." It was easy for him to see the relief fleeting across her oval honey-toned face. "Would you ever consider moving out there?"

Misha laughed and scooped up Ahmad. "What? And leave all this?" she called, while heading back to the living room. "I'm happy just visiting, thank you very much."

"Does that mean you'll join me?"

She settled the baby into the crib and didn't answer.

"What are you afraid of?" Talib folded his arms over the lightweight Cardinals sweatshirt he sported. "We've already slept together, you know."

Misha focused on the baby and tried to ignore that particular fact.

"Do you expect me to stay with you while we're there?"

"What sense would it make for you to stay elsewhere?" He smiled when she bristled. "I'd be happy to provide you with your own place if you insist."

Silently, Misha thought it was most likely she'd spend little time there. Besides, she said earlier that she'd travel whatever road to find out what she'd been denied all those years before. Here was her chance to prove that she meant it.

"All right, then," she said and almost laughed at his surprise. "Would you give the baby a bottle?" she asked en route to the kitchen.

"I saw Asher earlier. He didn't mention you watching the guy tonight." Talib observed her as she prepared the bottle.

Misha shrugged. "It all came up real fast for Riley and I…"

"Volunteered," he supplied, knowing full well her motivation behind the offer. Of course they both adored spending time with the little one. Still, he knew she was dead set against repeating another sexual event between them even though he knew in his gut that she wanted another, and more after that.

Misha began to heat the bottle. "So what time do we leave?"

Talib didn't respond and she turned to repeat the question. There was no need. His tongue was in her mouth seconds later and the moment met all the requirements for venturing well beyond the heated kiss.

His hand was beneath her top and cupping a breast while the other was massaging her center through the cottony pants.

Ahmad's tiny mewling broke the moment and had the godparents pulling apart as if they'd been caught doing something naughty.

"I'll be waiting for that." His dark eyes shifted toward the warming bottle.

Alone in the kitchen, Misha slumped back against the counter and prayed for strength.

Talib wouldn't have been surprised to have been told he'd smiled all throughout his sleep. Waking up to her hair teasing his nose with its scent and texture, her bare skin beneath his fingertips…he wanted this for a lifetime. This time, however, he wouldn't be dumb enough to lose it.

When he opened his eyes, his fate was sealed if it wasn't already. Misha rested on him, snuggled trustingly against his chest while Ahmad slept in the center of it. They'd fallen asleep on the quilted pallet Misha set up on the living-room floor where they'd played with the baby into the wee hours.

Yes, this was what he wanted—a life. Not stolen moments and discussions concocted through some work-related issue.

Misha stirred, her lashes fluttering and she looked right at him.

"I love you," he greeted simply, honestly.

She bit her lip, taking stock of their position.

Something stirred in her gaze when she saw Ahmad lying there against Talib.

"We should be getting up." She was already starting to brace against him. "Asher and Riley'll be here soon," she explained when his arm flexed about her.

Talib wanted to savor it all just a moment longer.

"Talib—"

He kissed her then and she whimpered, succumbing briefly before taking her will by the reins and pulling back. "I haven't even brushed my teeth." She uttered the first excuse that came to mind yet surrendered once again when he resumed their kiss.

When they pulled apart for the second time, it was to the sound of Ahmad giggling at the two of them. The baby's head bobbed up and down on Talib's chest.

"On that note…" Misha sighed.

She and Talib rose gingerly. Talib left the room to change the baby while Misha prepared a fresh bottle and listened to the guys while the bottle warmed in a pot on the stove.

"Just give it eight minutes," she called when he looked up from changing Ahmad and found her watching them. "It'll be ready. I'm going to grab a shower."

Ahmad cooed, bringing his godfather's thoughts back to reality.

"The bottle, right, mate."

"Arriving in our clothes from last night. Misha's gonna have a ball with this one," Riley purred as her husband nibbled her earlobe.

Asher chuckled. "Not as much of a ball as we had."

"Stop." She slapped his shoulder. "You know we could've come back last night for the baby."

"And rob her of all that fun? Some friend you are."

The Hudsons were engaged in a sultry kiss when the door opened before them.

"Ah…if it isn't Mummy and Daddums."

Surprised on several levels, Asher and Riley took a while to cross the threshold.

"Well, well…" Riley took Ahmad. "Did you see anything inappropriate last night, sweetie?" she asked her son.

Talib kissed Riley's temple. "He was the perfect witness—can't talk and doesn't know what 'inappropriate' means."

"Mmm-hmm. Let's go see what Aunty Misha has to say about that."

"It's not what you think," Talib said to Asher once Riley and the baby had gone to the back of the apartment.

Asher shrugged, though his brow rose in a devilish manner. "I was only thinking how sweet it was of you to help with the baby."

"I came over to ask about the trip." Talib looked pretty pleased with himself. "She agreed to come along."

"So you went with the bribery?"

Talib grinned. "Didn't have to. I simply reminded her of the kink this trip would put in our interviews for the story."

"Mmm-hmm…" Asher grunted, while searching Misha's fridge. "Bribery."

Talib waved off his friend and left the kitchen.

Misha was just wrapping into a towel when she heard Riley's voice.

"Why, Miss Bales, we'd have found another sitter had we known you were having a young man over."

"Riley, you scared me." Misha braced a hand to the bathroom doorjamb for support. "And it wasn't even like that."

"Please don't explain." Riley glanced across her shoulder. "I'd rather know what the suitcase is for."

"He asked me to go with him to Phoenix." Misha leaned against the dresser and pulled a scarf from her head.

"Wow." Riley toyed with Ahmad's tiny fists. "That's the last move I'd expect you to make, given all the tension."

"Oh, that." Misha dropped the scarf into a basket on the dresser. "We relieved a lot of *that tension* the other night."

Riley's mouth formed a perfect oval.

Misha collected Ahmad before his mother dropped him.

"So where do things stand now?" Riley finally managed a question.

"It was only sex, Riley."

"So what's your going to Phoenix really about?"

"The past." Misha sat on the edge of the bed and rocked the baby. "I've got to know more about his background. I'll do what's needed to get that story. As for all the rest—" her brows rose in a skeptical fashion "—I guess I'll just have to play by ear in handling all the rest."

Chapter 11

Phoenix, Arizona

Subdued was not a word Misha Bales would ever use while describing herself. It was a word she wouldn't even *think* of to describe herself.

She couldn't think of a *better* word to describe herself when she was escorted from the chopper that set down atop the roof of the Phoenix high-rise. She smiled demurely and thanked the young man for his assistance. When he moved on to collect the baggage, she turned her focus to Talib. He stood talking and laughing with the helicopter pilot and she accepted that for the time being she'd be completely out of her element.

She hadn't allowed herself much time to dwell on just how much he'd changed during the last six years.

Physically, there wasn't much difference. He was still gorgeous as hell with the added allure that men seemed to acquire in spades as they aged. No, this change had more to do with his persona. His demeanor had cooled and his words came more slowly and with more thought fueling them. Confidence was evident, but it wasn't tempered by anything cocky. This was just another more evolved part of who he'd become.

He was still speaking with the pilot, but noticed her staring and strolled toward her without breaking the conversation he held.

"Hungry?" Talib was asking once Misha had thanked the pilot for a great flight. "Should we eat out or stay in?"

Misha's brows rose as she debated. "It's all the same, isn't it? Considering…"

Talib threw his head back and laughed while Misha simply observed and admired.

"The building is home to many business people in the area," Talib explained later while they dined. "We all pay very dearly for that chopper service, but damn if it isn't a handy amenity."

"It's very impressive." Misha raked her nails across the sleeves of the aquamarine wrap dress she wore. "Have you lived here the entire time you've been in Phoenix?" She cast an appreciative stare toward the glossy cherry-wood furnishings of the restaurant.

Talib added more sauce to his T-bone and nodded. "Pretty much," he said.

Misha couldn't help but give a tiny shiver of happiness. The softly lit elegant warmth of their surroundings instilled contentment and every other soothing emotion she could conjure. She sipped more wine and continued her survey of the establishment.

Talib had decided on dinner at the eatery the building boasted. *Business people have lots of business dinners,* he'd said in defense of yet another pricey amenity.

They'd dined heartily, and that, combined with the conversation, added an even more enjoyable element to the outing. It wasn't long, though, before Misha's curiosity reared its head.

"So is damage control the usual with this client of yours?"

Talib spoke around a corner of steak. "Actually, Asher and I are a couple of the lucky ones—we've been pretty good judges of character. Rarely do we pick a bad apple...rarely."

Misha's thoughts reflected on Ray Simmons, the "bad apple" who'd signaled the start of their troubles. Quickly, she realized the topic was probably not the best for them to embark upon.

"Talib, this restaurant is really nice—"

"I came to the hospital that night."

She immediately went silent.

"Linda, your assistant...she told me about the accident."

That was definitely not the subject change Misha wanted. "We shouldn't—"

"We'd have been together three years that day and

I kicked myself all day over how far out of hand I'd let things go." Losing taste for the food, he dropped his napkin across the plate. "I've been kicking myself since I first accused you, actually."

She bristled. "And yet you continued."

"And yet I continued. You see…I had to be right about you."

"Because of my background."

"Humph, because of *my* background."

"Yes?" She so wanted him to continue, but he was clearly set on discussing the accident.

"I'd gone to your flat to apologize—used my key—" he grimaced on the memory "—the place was a mess. I tried your cell but there was no answer." He massaged his shoulder through the coffee fabric of his shirt. "Calling Linda was a last resort."

Misha settled against the cushioned back of the chair and listened.

"You looked so tiny in that bed. Tinier than usual." He smirked, then and raked his stare across her body. "I was responsible."

"No." She leaned close to the table's edge. "No, Talib—"

"I didn't put you in the car…but I was at fault just the same."

Misha reached across the table and squeezed his hand. "Why are you so set on that?"

Gently, he pulled free of her hold. Standing, he dropped several bills to the table.

"Let's get out of here."

* * *

For the second time that day, Misha gave into that subdued feeling. Talib's condo was almost a replica of the man himself—dark, elegant and appealing. It was a place that urged meditation and rejuvenation. The earth tones meshed with other rich, dark coloring, creating a mellow quality that had Misha walking through the place as if led by some invisible thread.

"It's lovely," she breathed, feeling his eyes on her seconds before she turned and actually saw him watching while he followed her deeper into his home.

She turned off into the den and Talib grimaced, hoping she'd continue on down the long curving corridor that ended at his bedroom.

In the den, Misha took note of the pictures lining the walls, mantel, shelving and tables. She tried to maintain her cool by focusing on the pictures featuring people she didn't recognize.

"Your family?" Her voice was light and she glanced up in time to catch his nod.

She noticed the same two men in many of the photos and paused to more closely study one of them.

"My uncles," he said, well aware what picture resided in the frame she held.

"You must be very close." Carefully, she replaced the frame on the mantel.

"They raised me."

"Oh." Misha was observing other photos along the pine mantelpiece. "With your mother?"

"My mother was dead."

She whirled around to question him, but cried out instead when she realized he'd come up quickly and silently behind her.

Questions then were *out* of the question. Talib was kissing her with a force that had as much to do with arousal as it did with frustration and the need to silence demons that were not quite ready to be shared. Misha could practically feel the emotions surging through him like live beings.

He lifted her next to him and she gasped. "I can't stay."

"We'll see about that." His mouth was smoothing a path beneath her jaw. Infrequently, his teeth grazed her silken skin, lightly scented with her heavenly fragrance.

Misha whimpered, kicking off her peekaboo pumps and draping her legs around his back. Hungry for him, she wasted no time working to remove his shirt. Talib's intentions ran along the same track. By the time they reached his bedroom, both he and Misha were half out of their clothing.

The room was dark and Misha felt herself being lowered, then covered, by his heavy frame. She wouldn't let him claim total control this time and pushed him to his back. She'd see him totally nude before she was.

"Misha…" Talib allowed himself to be handled and massaged the heels of his hands into his eyes while savoring the feel of her mouth gliding across his neck and shoulders. Her nails grazed his chest and abdomen with an underlying yet noticeable air of possession.

Her tongue tickled his navel while she undid his trouser fastening. Talib's moan held a wavering quality then and he wasn't in the least bit shamed by it. She had him undressed and her mouth trailed steadily downward until her lips favored the length of his sex. Her tongue darted out to add another level of heat to the caress. She settled her hands to his powerful thighs when they bucked in involuntary thrusts as she pleasured him. She dropped kisses across the tops of his legs and smiled at the sight of him writhing in unsatisfied need.

At last, she granted his wish and rose up to cover him. Misha's intent was to kiss him but the instant she lay across him he sat up. His arms were around her waist, holding her close. He massaged her back even as he drew her closer to suckle her ever-firming nipples.

Misha was so lost in the sensation of it all, she whimpered and enacted the same bucking movements with her hips that he had earlier.

Talib was fumbling for a condom, but halted the search when he surrendered to the craving for her nipple against his tongue. The sleek lines of his brows drew close as he licked and suckled madly before his nose outlined the circumference of a firm breast and he suckled it all over again.

"Talib…" Misha's voice was more air than tone.

Talib was again in search of a condom. Once located and unwrapped, he eased it in place with Misha twisting and bouncing against him in desire and anticipation.

Her forehead nudged his when he settled her down to sheath his erection. Misha's tiny whimpering gained volume, but soon enough the room filled with both of their satisfied cries. She lost her fingers in his gorgeous hair and winced as every bounce upon his length nestled him deeper inside.

Talib resumed his ravenous feasting on her breasts. He cupped one, manipulating the nipple between thumb and forefinger while his lips and tongue tended to the other.

"Talib…coming…mmm….soon…" she warned.

He pushed her to her back and took her with more determination. Her shrieks of pleasure though, made him pause.

"Am I hurting you?"

"Never."

His head fell to her shoulder and he smiled. He knew she was in the throes of desire and that her response to his inquiry wasn't in the literal sense. Still…he could pretend. He could pretend that she truly believed he'd never hurt her. That he'd never hurt her again.

Talib was up and fully dressed before Misha even awoke the next morning. He ordered breakfast, but didn't dare wake her for it. He enjoyed his food while watching her rest. The sight of her in his bed admittedly fed his ego while it nourished his heart. He'd do whatever it took not to lose this, lose her. Once again, she'd become his lifeline. He wondered if she'd ever really been anything less.

He felt his phone vibrating against the table and smirked when he saw the name on the screen.

"Claudette, good morning."

"Everything's set for your meeting with Ducker."

Talib poured himself more juice. "And he knows I'm not coming to his hotel?"

"He knows." Claudette chuckled. "It was heavenly letting him know you were out here to see him. I think the little prince was a tad bit intimidated."

"Humph, we'll see." Talib swallowed the juice in a gulp.

Claudette's chuckling resumed. "Understood. I've got the straight jacket and muzzle beneath my desk, just in case."

"That a girl," Talib commended.

"Oh, and don't let this drama with Duck cause you to forget the event for the Arizona Orchestra."

"What about it?" Talib tilted his head, hoping to capture a glimpse of something when Misha turned onto her back.

"The charity concert? It's this week and since Asher's back East…"

Talib suddenly lost his taste for the rest of breakfast. "The fun is all mine," he grudgingly acknowledged.

"Sorry, *mate*," Claudette teased.

He smirked. "Watch it."

"Seriously, Talib, you're going to have to get past this aversion to parties. 'It's an integral part to an agent's success,' as Asher likes to say."

"Asher also likes parties more than I do."

"Honey, a hermit crab likes parties more than you

do. Just show your handsome face for a second or three, all right?"

"I'll see what I can do." He pushed away the table cart and stood. "Talk to you soon."

Misha was stirring and opened her eyes to find Talib stooping near the bed. "Nice suit." She smoothed a hand across the fabric of the sandstone three-piece. "Should I get dressed?"

Talib held a card key between his index and middle fingers. "I'd prefer you stay just like that until I get back, but if you're hell-bent—" he wiggled the key "—there's a suite waiting for you right here in the building."

She smiled. "Another amenity?"

"Of course." His tone was lighthearted enough but his expression was all seriousness. He studied her sleep-softened face and tousled hair. "I'll be back by three. Will you be all right until then?" He nodded once she did.

"There's breakfast." He glanced toward the cart. "I ordered a while ago so…you may want something different and…"

Misha wondered if he knew he was rambling. Probably not, for he appeared more interested in stroking her hair than in the words coming out of his mouth.

"So I'll see you at three?" she said once his words trailed into silence.

He gave her a sheepish smile, kissed her nose and was gone.

Chapter 12

"So how's the baby business?" Misha was asking later that day when the receptionist connected her call through to Dr. Lettia Breene.

"Girl! How are things?" The obstetrician laughed. "We're gonna have to get together for lunch or something—maybe get Riley to come along so we can all catch up."

"That sounds good…." Misha ran her finger along the mouth of the coffee mug she stroked. "Might be a little difficult to get together from Phoenix, though."

"Phoenix? A story?"

"Talib."

"Ah…so, um, when do you think you'll be back?"

"I went along when he asked because I was curious, Lett."

Lettia was silent.

Misha pushed aside the coffee she'd been enjoying from the living room of the suite Talib had secured for her. "He's so set on taking the blame for what happened six years ago."

"Well, that's nothing new," Lettia said. "He felt that way from the night of your accident."

"And I've got a strong feeling that need to take the blame goes straight to his background. Or at least it plays a role in it."

"A person's background can haunt them for years." Lettia voiced the point in a softer tone. "Will you be as honest with Talib as he's been with you?"

Misha straightened on the sofa, at first confused.

"Things got pretty bad for you after the accident."

The confusion cleared. "Are you crazy?" Laughter flavored Misha's words but they lacked humor. "There's no way I could tell him that. Maybe before. *Maybe,* but not now."

"Honey, isn't it time for honesty? Full disclosure, if you will—on both sides."

"Talib has this need to take the blame for everything, Lett. How do I tell him all about that and not have him add it to the list of things he thinks he's responsible for?"

"I think he could be coming clean because he wants a life with you. You need to ask yourself if that's what *you* want, and if so, how will you explain your sessions with Dr. Zeitz?"

Misha cursed.

"Talib's too smart to believe you're just seeing a therapist because of an accident."

"He knows my mind was a mess after all that happened between us that day," Misha argued, picking at a thread on the cuff of her jeans. "Lots of people see therapists for things like that. I won't ever need to talk about this with anyone except you and Dr. Z."

"How long will you guys be out there?"

"I'm not sure," Misha sighed, leaving the sofa to take in the view from the tall windows lining the room. "Talib seems pretty content—he got me settled in a room to die for."

"You think you'll have the full story by the end of your trip?"

"I hope so. He gets so clammy when he starts talking about it." Misha puffed out her cheeks and sat on the back of an armchair. "Especially when he starts talking about his mother."

"Mother?" Intrigue laced Lettia's voice.

"Things were pretty hard for them…before she died."

"Which explains him clamming up."

"I don't know, Lett." Misha was back before the windows again. "I can't figure what it is, only that I think it's something he believes is his fault."

Lettia sighed. "Sounds like it's getting complicated, Meesh."

"More so every day."

"Can you handle that?"

"I love him. I never stopped. I don't have a choice but to see it through."

Following her phone call with Lettia, Misha enjoyed what remained of her day. She didn't leave the suite at all and couldn't recall when she'd last enjoyed such alone time. The place was stocked with everything she could want or need. She commended Talib's thoughtfulness, certain he'd arranged every detail. Lately he seemed to have his finger on the pulse of all her needs—literally.

Thankfully, her *needs* now were only a touch or a cup of her favorite tea away. She remembered when her cravings were much harder to satisfy, much more dangerous.

Closing her eyes then, she sank deeper into the bubble-filled tub. Surely a nice hot bath would soothe those troubled memories.

It was difficult to follow the order to relax at first. Soon though, the bath foam's wonderful fragrance worked its magic. Far too soon, almost an hour had passed and Misha had no intentions of leaving. Feeling truly decadent, she inched deeper into the tub and prepared for a second hour. She was lifting her legs in and out of the water, watching the suds stream down one limb and then the other. A low wolf whistle stopped her mid-lift a moment or so later. Water sloshed when she saw Talib in the doorway.

"Does everyone have a key to these private suites?"

She worked to catch her breath while eyeing him warily.

Talib shrugged, one hand hidden in the pocket of his trousers while the other fingered the key. "I'm the only one," he promised.

Misha swallowed, the sound of his accented tone seeming to vibrate amidst the bathroom. "Don't suppose there's anything I could do to get it back?"

Talib smirked, easing the key into his coat pocket while advancing beyond the door. "There're several things you might do to get it back."

"I'll bet." She laughed faintly when he kneeled near the tub. Absently, he began trailing the back of his hand along her shoulder.

"Need help?" He offered as his touch journeyed toward the swell of her breasts barely covered by the rapidly fading bubbles.

"I can handle it." She shook her head.

Talib made a tsking sound and his ebony gaze narrowed sharply. "I fear you've been handling too much on your own."

Misha was quiet, only watching as he unbuttoned his shirt cuffs and rolled the sleeves above muscular forearms. She blinked when the clatter of his wristwatch against the counter drew her back to reality. "I, um…I don't have much choice in that, do I?"

"Mmm…there's always a choice." His unbuttoned vest followed the watch to the counter. "Especially when there's someone eager to offer assistance."

Her lashes batted madly when his fingers drifted

around the curve of her breast, down her breasts, lower...
She bit her lip when an unexpected cry lilted from her
throat. Her legs were parting on their own accord in
response to his infrequent grazes against her thighs.

"There just some things a girl has to handle on her
own," she said.

"Some things." His eyes were focused on the water.
"Not everything." His thumb applied a sinful massage
to her sex.

Misha almost slid beneath the water. Instead, she
pressed her lips together and closed her hands over
the tub's beige porcelain edge. Giving in, she took
the probing caress allowing her legs to part in silent
invitation for more. In moments, Talib's hands had her
calling out for him not to stop. She was cursing herself
in moments, when he did, in fact, stop. His hand rose
up and out of the water, fingers trailing her jaw before
he left her alone in the bathroom.

Misha was moving to pull the water plug when Talib
returned. She was too weakened by the sight of him to
do anything other than take in the sight of his body,
thoroughly nude and fully erect. Her mouth went dry.
He mentioned something about her needing more water
and hit the knob.

"Talib—"

"Shall I leave?"

"Please, no." She averted her gaze yet smiled when
he tossed down a condom.

Setting aside the package, Misha rose to her knees
and grazed her nose along the powerful chords in his

heavy thighs. The caress ventured upward along his rigid length, pulsing with arousal. Her mouth covered him, giving her a shrill of delight when he groaned. Misha held him snugly, working her mouth along his length until *he* begged her to take things to the next level.

With protection firmly in place, Talib wasted no time with foreplay. Misha braced her hands behind her on the bottom of the tub when he gripped a thigh, holding her secure as he claimed her.

The sight of their reflections in the mirror roused a sharp cry from Misha's lips. Shallow light radiated in from the bedroom and provided an intriguing shadow. Misha swallowed around her heart lodged in her throat. The powerful vision of him kneeling above as he thrust relentlessly inside her rushed the sensation of sheer bliss through her body.

Misha threw back her head, so overwhelmed by sensation then that she couldn't even gasp. Before either of them could reach release, Talib withdrew. He repositioned Misha effortlessly and took her from behind. She was orgasmic the second he added his mouth to the act, working his lips and perfect teeth across her shoulders as he continued to lunge until they both came to a shattering release.

Afterward, the lovers lounged in the tub of tepid and clear water. They felt more content than ever. Misha raked her fingers across the unyielding curves of Talib's sculpted pecs. Her thumbnail raked one nipple while her lips brushed the other.

"How'd it go with your client?" she asked.

"Humph. Ducker Conrad." Talib brushed a hand across his damp curls and grimaced. "Kid thinks he's entitled to having it easy because he came up hard."

"Mmm…" Misha focused on the engravings decorating the bath tiles. "I grew up with a lot of people like that. Hell, I was like that," she said with a chuckle. "Then, I finally got it. Nobody was gonna give me a damn thing just 'cause I expected it."

"And you've put your finger right on Mr. Conrad's problem." Talib smirked while massaging the bridge of his nose. "It's a damn shame anyway. It's not difficult to see why he's having such trouble—kid had all the makings of a great childhood. Just wasn't meant to be. Unfortunately, nobody warned him of that part."

Misha inched up, taking in his expression as she moved. She wondered how much of that explanation reflected on Talib himself. "So did he grow up that hard?" she asked, hoping in turn to obtain more information about the man she rested against.

Talib rubbed the small of her back and sighed. "Not in the way you think, though. His family's financially sound. His dad owns a place on the outskirts of Tucson—incredible ranch."

"So what happened?"

"Family problems."

Fascinated, Misha watched the muscles flex in Talib's chest when he tensed over the answer.

"Things ended tragically. Ducker didn't take it well

at all. He was no more than twelve or thirteen, but it can take a lifetime to get past some things."

"Especially if you keep them to yourself?"

Further conversation was silenced. Talib was kissing her and it didn't take Misha long to realize their talk was over. She braced against his chest, but Talib kept the upper hand, driving his tongue voraciously against hers. Misha was soon past any arguments and Talib must have sensed that, for he eventually broke the kiss and filled his mouth with her breast.

Misha was limp with need and feared she'd slip right beneath the surface of the water. Talib's fingers inside her and his tongue turning her nipples into rigid gems had her thoughts wholly centered on him and the pleasure he stoked.

Effortlessly, Talib lifted her from the tub. Dripping wet, they fell to the center of the bed and loved each other for hours.

Misha lay in the center of the bed, taking in deep gulps of air, following the explicit scene that had just occurred. Talib wasn't wasting time catching his breath. He hadn't stopped working over her since she'd collapsed minutes earlier.

A beautifully sculpted mouth traveled the length of her—leaving no spot untouched. He ventured lower, and, despite her worn-out state, Misha felt her sex clench when his teeth grazed the bare triangle of skin above it.

Talib moved on, though, grazing the top of her thigh then and down before he stopped. Misha felt him squeeze her leg and give it a turn. She opened her eyes to find him inspecting her knee.

"From the accident," she said, marveling at how well he actually remembered her body.

For seconds, he was still. Only his thumb brushed the scar. He released her and slowly pushed up.

"We could probably use something to eat."

Misha bit her lip to keep from saying what was at the tip of her tongue. Talib left the bed, quietly exiting the room.

Chapter 13

"You all right?"

Misha tightened the peach bandana that kept the hair from her face. "Yeah, why?"

"You've barely said a word since we set out."

"Well, I've never seen this part of Arizona." Misha turned to look out the passenger window of the F150 truck Talib drove. "Phoenix is beautiful, but this—" she waved her hand past the window where the Sonoran Desert whizzed by "—this is awesome. Where're we heading, anyway?"

"Does it matter?"

It didn't and that was the honest truth. At that moment, Misha believed she'd go anywhere he asked.

"I just can't imagine anything civilized being out here," she clarified when he looked over at her.

Talib chuckled, flexing his fingers on the wheel. "Well, that depends on your idea of civilized."

"True," Misha laughed, and then shrugged. "It's just that most people wouldn't give up all the comforts for desolation and remoteness no matter how lovely it is."

Talib leaned his head on the headrest. "Are you counting yourself among that lot?"

Misha's brows rose as she considered the question. "No, no, I'm not." The response was genuine and even surprised her a little. "I think in spite of my upbringing, I could really do without seeing twenty million people every day."

"The city girl longing for a country life, eh?"

"I'm not longing." She rested her head against the padded rest. "There is something…hypnotic about it all, though." Her sparkling dark eyes traveled from the voluminous clouds filling the sky to the mountain ranges in the distance. The windows were down and even the air held a crispness, an aliveness, that she wanted to soak in.

Ten minutes later, Talib was turning the truck down a dirt road. At least, Misha figured, it was an actual road. Every path they'd taken that morning had been pretty much dirt-laden. She saw a sign that was decorated by a double set of horseshoes on either side of two elegant capitalized letter *C*'s.

"C.C.?" she inquired when they passed beneath the sign.

"Conrad Cove."

It didn't take long to make the connection. "Ducker Conrad."

Talib nodded.

"Is this the best idea?"

"Why, whatever do you mean, love?"

"I mean, you can't possibly be this dense." Misha lifted her chin when he slanted her a look. "This is your business, Talib. I shouldn't be interfering. I'm guessing this won't be a party."

"You're not interfering. You're accompanying."

"It all comes down to the same thing and I really don't need to be there." She folded her arms over her chest and flopped back on the seat. "I sure as hell don't need you worried that this will wind up in a story."

"Shedding a little light on the situation might do Duck's ass a little good, actually. Everyone will know what a jackass he's being." He grinned. "Hold that thought. *The Chronicle* may be in for a scoop."

"Talib—"

"Do you happen to recall our agreement?"

Sharp as ever, Misha pursed her lips as memory served. "Whatever you say, Talib."

"That's more like it."

The lengthy dirt road eventually ended at what Misha could only describe as an oasis. Aside from the unexpected Mediterranean-style home in the distance, the area was filled by an unexpected expanse of green and was fenced by trees.

A few horses roamed the front and far sides of the

house. Misha could see various buildings spanning the property beyond the living area. All was encased in a simple white fence that appeared to run on into oblivion.

"How?" was all Misha could ask, looking from the property to Talib.

He didn't need clarification. "Blaine Conrad can make anything grow, or so it's rumored."

Misha leaned close to the window, eyeing her surroundings with a mix of apprehension and curiosity. Absently, she accepted Talib's hand when he came around the truck and opened her door. She followed quietly while he led the way. Moments before they breached the privacy fence, she braced against him, prepared to argue her case again.

Talib turned, cupping Misha's face as he leaned down to look straight into her eyes. "I need you with me here, all right?"

"It's your business, Talib. Mixing that with me hasn't worked too well for us, you know?" She looked down.

"I need you in there, love. Can't that be enough?"

Misha searched his dark eyes with hers and smiled at what she saw. He pressed a hard kiss to her forehead when she nodded.

"For better or worse, Blaine Conrad, Ducker's father, is a real ladies' man," Talib explained once he and Misha were headed toward the house again. "Our conversation is likely to get tense. With you there—" he squeezed her "—perhaps we can still make a little headway."

"You're a sexist, Mr. Mason."

Talib shrugged. "Sue me."

"Pretty face on hand or not, the man's not going to like having a stranger overhearing his family business." She frowned, not liking the look Talib was giving her when their steps drew to a halt.

"Stranger?" He laughed softly, and then kissed the back of her hand before they fell into step again.

The couple was met by a tiny, round Hispanic woman whom Talib called Armelita and greeted with a warm hug and kiss. He turned toward Misha and the little woman's eyes brightened.

"Is this Misha?" she asked, her rich brown eyes twinkling in wonder.

Misha gasped, her eyes flying to Talib's face before she looked back at the tiny woman. Remembering her manners, she extended her hand for a shake but found herself drawn into a hug instead.

Curiosity far outreaching apprehension then, Misha wanted answers. They'd have to wait. She and Talib were being bustled into the house but Misha could scarcely appreciate the loveliness of it all especially when Blaine Conrad came out to greet them.

Although older, Blaine was as tall as Talib and just as well built. Talib had called him a ladies' man and Misha could very well believe it. His face was handsome and weather-beaten. He was clearly a sun worshipper, which was understandable given his line of work. The brilliance of an even white smile was a dazzling contrast against his tanned skin and sun-bleached blond hair.

"Is this Misha?" Blaine asked when he and Talib hugged.

"How is it that I'm so well known?" Misha felt she'd kept her curiosity quiet long enough.

"Talib's a frequent visitor to our humble digs," Blaine explained, having walked over to drop an arm across her shoulders. "He and I have had many discussions over many things. Especially the things that mean the most to us." He tossed a wink toward Talib. "This guy's mentioned you more times than I can count."

Misha would've expected Talib to change the conversation or at least look away when she fixed him with a questioning stare. But he met her gaze evenly as though daring her to argue with how much she meant to him then.

"So, T, is this a Ducker visit or a fun one?" Blaine's question saved the moment from turning too charged. His sky blue gaze twinkled as he observed Misha.

She laughed. *Ladies' man, indeed.*

Talib wasn't quite as amused. "It's definitely a Ducker visit."

Blaine's expression soured a bit. "Then this'll require drinks." He offered Misha his arm. "What's your poison, beauty?"

Talib hung back, watching the two walk off into the shadowed interior of the house. If things worked according to plan, there'd be more than talk over Blaine Conrad's angry son.

Conrad Cove was the place he came to think, to reflect and to *plan*. His intention was to use the time to finally share with Misha what he'd been unable to for far too long. He only prayed his emotions and his own storage of anger and hate wouldn't get the better of him.

Grimacing just slightly, Talib headed off into the house.

"You need to talk to your son."

"It's a waste of time, his and mine," Blaine said once Talib had shared Ducker's latest dilemma. "No way is that boy ever going to forgive me for what happened between his mother and me."

Misha's gaze snapped to Talib's face, but he was all business.

Blaine tossed back the rest of his bourbon. "And until he does, there's no way he's gonna listen to me about a damn thing, including his football career."

"He'll listen, Blaine. I truly believe this may be the one way to get through to him, and if you think about it, it's the one thing we haven't tried." Talib leaned over and brought a hand down on Blaine's knee. "He needs you. That kid can push and shove everyone else away but *you're* his dad. You can shove as hard as he can. You *should* shove as hard as he can."

"I pray you'll never have to see hate in your son's eyes, Talib," Blaine said as he rose from the sofa and paced the den. "It's perhaps one of the few things in the world even a strong man can't stomach—hate lurking in your child's stare." He went to toss back more bourbon and realized the glass was empty. "I've seen that from Duck more times that I can count."

"You can change that."

"How, Talib?"

"You love him."

"And love conquers all."

"Sometimes, yes." Talib shrugged. "As it relates to a parent and child, I'd say definitely yes."

"He won't go for it."

Talib leaned back in the armchair he occupied. "We've arranged for him to meet with the team execs. I told him what I expected of him, save for the fact that you might be there."

Blaine turned. "And?"

"He didn't argue." Talib smirked. "Of course, that was probably because he's too afraid of me to do so. But if we can use that fear to open up some communication between the two of you—why not?"

Blaine looked hopeful but still felt too jaded to let that hope mislead him. "Talib, do you really believe in your gut that my boy will talk to me?"

"If my father gave a damn enough about me to come see me through rough times, I'd be interested enough to hear what he has to say."

Misha was riveted by Talib, whose expression then gave away more than he probably realized. Just then, Armelita came in to offer a tour of the house. Feeling it best to give the men their privacy, Misha accepted.

"So did you bring her here to share things you should've already told her?" Blaine queried once the women were gone.

"I've been trying to work my way up to it." Talib

shook his head and looked out the glass doors across the room. "Been trying to work my way up to it for a bloody long time."

"And this is kind of like the preamble?"

Talib grinned. "I guess. Hell, Blaine, I don't know what the devil I'm doing. I don't do too well talking about this. It pisses me off just to think about how the past still affects me. I'm a grown man, for Christ's sake." He leaned forward to rub his hands across his head. "She deserves the truth, though. I owe it to her—all of it."

Blaine perched on the back of the leather sofa. "So you expect to get her back afterward."

"I have her back now."

Blaine smiled, approving of the younger man's confidence.

"When I start talking of the past though—" Talib flexed a fist "—I wonder if I deserve her."

"Don't do that, son. You've gone too long without her—don't second-guess yourself now."

Talib knew Blaine was right. "It just doesn't make it easier, you know?"

"This I know all too well." Blaine chuckled.

Talib joined in on the laughter. "We're quite a pair."

Blaine went to refill his drink at the pine bar in the corner of the den. "So how long will it take for you to talk with her now that she's here?" he asked.

"Being here helps." Talib stood and walked over to the glass doors. "When I think about it…it makes me so damn mad and then she's right there and…"

Smirking, Blaine passed his friend a fresh drink. "Talking is the last thing on your mind?" he guessed.

"She's like a drug." Talib studied the burgundy liquid filling the glass. "She's always been that way to me."

Blaine clapped Talib's back once he'd joined him at the doors. "That's something you sure as hell don't want to lose."

Talib and Blaine caught up to Misha and Armelita toward the end of the house tour. Afterward, the group went on a riding tour of the grounds. Misha commended herself on handling horseback, crediting her abilities to the trip out to Victor Lyne's ranch the previous year.

It was past lunch time when the outdoor tour ended, but Talib had another area he wanted to share with Misha before they settled down to a meal.

The now familiar subdued feeling plagued Misha again, only this time there was also contentment. The dwelling Talib led them to was sheltered behind a wealth of trees much like the ones shielding the main house.

It was extraordinary, yet comforting, to find such shade amidst a desert oasis. Talib helped her from the amber-colored mare and kept hold of Misha's hand while leading her toward the house there.

"So who are we meeting now?" Misha faked playfulness to mask how nervous she was.

"Only the two of us here, love." His regal tone held a hushed quality. "The guesthouse is only open to me. It's where I spend much of my time when I'm not handling business in Phoenix."

Again, Misha's eyes were wide in purveyance of her surroundings. "I thought you lived in Phoenix."

"I *work* in Phoenix." He checked his chain for the key. "I come out here to get away from all that."

"Humph, I see how it is. Some of us go to our apartments, while some of us have heavenly escapes to enjoy," she teased, but sobered when he suddenly brought her hand to his chest.

"It hasn't been heaven until now."

Gently, Misha extracted her hand and ventured beyond the threshold when the door opened. She shouldn't have been surprised to know he came here for rejuvenation.

The man held a fondness for soft lighting, that was for sure. The place was cozy and awash with a palate of earth tones. Elaborate sculptures and paintings decorated the space. The pieces were lit with just the right sort of illumination to draw an onlooker's eye toward each creation while accentuating the background of the room. Exotic cacti and other flowers indigenous to the area filled the cottage.

"You're *very* lucky in your real estate acquisitions, Mr. Mason." She folded her arms across the scoop bodice of her peach T-shirt and turned toward him. "Now I'm hoping you didn't bring me here for a tour or anything physical," she added when he advanced. "Unless it's talking."

Talib's expression rivaled his eyes for darkness and he walked off toward the bar.

"How long will we dance to this song, Tali?" She leaned next to the sofa. "If it makes you feel better then by all means we can certainly talk under the pretense of the story." She smiled when he whirled around to face her.

"You're about ten times as private as Asher. Exactly how long did you expect me to buy that you'd allow any of what you told me so far to wind up in a paper?" She rounded the sofa and selected a place to recline. "So let's talk, Mr. Mason. And fix me a drink while you're at it."

Chapter 14

Over drinks and salads, Talib and Misha settled down in the living room. At first, the sounds of pepper grinding and utensils cutting into veggies were all that filled the room. Two bites into the salad, Talib began to talk about how he'd met Blaine Conrad.

"I talked to my uncles about wanting to go to school in America. They suggested I visit first just to be sure. I still had no idea where I wanted to study once I got here. My uncles arranged for me to come and stay with Blaine and Ducker—who was only eleven or twelve at the time. My uncles breed horses and met Blaine years ago—they were all great friends."

Talib helped himself to another forkful of the zesty Southwestern salad. "Blaine was happy to have me here.

Duck needed someone closer to his age, so to speak, with all that had happened with his mum."

Misha focused on picking through her salad. "What happened there?" she asked, fearing Talib would clam up again when he didn't continue right away.

"Blaine once took his crown of ladies' man very seriously. It didn't much matter that he was married." Talib washed down the salad with a swig of liquor. "One night his wife had enough. She caught him out in the stables. Ducker never forgave his dad."

Misha set her salad dish to the coffee table. "While you and Blaine were talking, I got the feeling that there were some similarities there."

Talib winced, as if losing taste for his salad, as well. "I don't know how much of a ladies' man my father was, but he screwed up royally with my mum."

"Will you tell me?"

"He swept my mother off her feet. She fell in love." He leaned forward, focusing on rubbing his hands together. "All she wanted was to be a wife and mother. Her family didn't like it, or my dad, for that matter. When I was old enough to ask about it, she'd only say 'when a woman's in love…'"

Misha smiled. She understood that phrase all too well.

"We were a happy family, I thought. Until my dad's assistant wanted to be more than his assistant." His rubbing hands turned into flexing fists. "I'd hear my mum crying, trying to argue, screaming for someone to stop calling and then screaming at my dad, demanding answers." He propped an elbow to his knee and rested his chin on his fist. "One day the woman came to the house and said Dad was hers. She said a bunch of other stuff and my mother just stood there…I don't think I understood all of what was going on, but I knew I wanted my mother to stop crying. I wanted us to leave him so she'd stop being upset all the time. But she said dad was a good provider and we needed him." He squeezed his eyes shut against the pressure of tears behind them.

"Then one day he didn't come home. Mum got an envelope filled with money a few days later. It paid the bills for a month." He smiled sourly. "Then she had to get a job, and with the few skills she had, well, it wasn't much of a job."

Misha realized her fingers were curled tight into the sofa cushions. She was forcing herself to remain seated when all she wanted was to go to him. It tore at her heart to see him rubbing at the moisture in his eyes.

"We made it for a while." He inhaled as though drawing in strength. "We had to move several times as our flats became too expensive. There were nights we didn't have food because the utilities had to be paid or we didn't have utilities because we were hungry as hell."

"But her family…" Misha scooted forward on the chair.

Talib nodded. "One night, I was about twelve, I think. She bundled me up, packed my clothes and we took a train ride." His stare softened as the memories grew more vivid. "I was excited because we didn't do extravagant things like that. We even had dinner on the train. Afterward, we walked a long walk, but it felt good on a full stomach." He stroked his jaw. "A maid answered the door Mum knocked on. The woman looked like she'd seen a ghost when she saw my mother. I'd never been inside a house that big. I'd *seen* plenty…" A grin emerged. "When I discovered *I* was going to live there…I met my uncles that night and they terrified me." He laughed and fell back against his chair.

"They looked scary and stern as hell, but the first thing out of my uncle Baron's mouth was a joke and then my uncle Cafrey was asking if I liked pumpkin ice cream. The maid had brought a crap-load and they couldn't stand the shite."

Misha burst into laughter.

"That's exactly the way he said it, I swear!" Talib's laughter rumbled a few seconds longer before it began to taper. "Mum laughed, even. So we had some of the ice cream in the living room before the fire. Then mum was kissing and hugging me and the maid was taking me to a room. I was so worn out I didn't argue, couldn't even get my head around the fact that the room was mine."

He massaged his forearms, visible beneath the short sleeves of his black polo top. "The next morning I woke up happy for the first time in so long. I got dressed and raced downstairs looking for my uncles and my mother. I found my uncles. But Mum was gone. She left me with them. They told me she said she couldn't stay." He held his face in his hands for a moment. "Weeks passed…then the police came calling one evening—told my uncles they'd found her on a cot at a soup house. She was…she was dead."

"Talib," Misha whispered and moved to go to him but he stood and turned away so she wouldn't see his face streaked with tears. "Talib, I'm so sorry…."

"So you see the background you think I'm so removed from—I know it quite well."

Misha stood behind him, studying his back, broad and tense with frustration. "Why would you think that any of what you've gone through made any of what happened between the two of us your fault?"

Talib braced his hands to the bar and bowed his head. "When that story came out six years ago, all I could think of was the woman who took my father away from my mother and I. I remembered her standing there in my mother's kitchen telling her she could never keep a man like my father. She said my mother had nothing to offer, nothing to talk about except the bills or what little Tali did at school. My father needed a career woman, she said. A woman who'd do what it took to be someone—a woman who'd do whatever it took to have it all."

Misha had taken a seat on the coffee table and pulled the bandana from her head in order to clench her hair between her fingers. She was shuddering as it all fell into place.

"I let that ruin what we had," he was saying. "I let the image of that woman and what she was turn me cold and angry and unwilling to listen to anything you had to say." He turned to look at her then. "*That's* why I can say it was my fault, Misha. I put you in that hospital bed the same way I put my mother in her grave."

Misha left the table and walked around in front of him. She caught the hem of his top when he would have turned his back again. "You've got no right to do that. Your mother wouldn't want you taking blame for something like that."

"You didn't know her," Talib snapped, rolling his eyes toward the ceiling. "You have no idea what she'd been through, killing herself to support me."

"I know she was your mother." Misha grabbed his forearm and squeezed until he looked at her. "I know no mother worth a damn would want her child blaming himself for something like that."

Unfortunately, Talib was beyond hearing anything Misha said then. "It's getting late. We should be going."

She dropped his arm. "Do we have to leave? I—I was hoping we could stay the night." She knew a long drive was the last thing either of them needed.

Talib was already shaking his head. "You're better off in your suite. Thank you for insisting on it."

Misha didn't want to be apart that night. Not with him being so out of sorts. "I'd feel better if we were together." She winced at the lost tone in her words.

He was kissing her senseless before she could speak another syllable and had her half out of her bra before he withdrew.

"That's the only thing you can expect from me tonight, so get your things and let's go."

Knowing he was in a frightful mood, Misha took her unease firmly in hand. "I don't want to leave," she cried out when he grabbed her fast, jerking her into another kiss that was far hungrier than the last.

Misha could feel his frustration coming through in the kiss much like the other times he'd been affected by talk of the past. Her heart beat triple time in her throat yet she surrendered to what he needed, overcome by the passion of his desire. She could hear the low, growling sounds he uttered as his mouth took possession of hers. His hands roamed with mastery and desire entwined.

Talib helped her to the floor and took Misha out of her clothes. Her whimpers filled the room in response to his mouth and his fingers left no spot untouched on her body. He scooped her up then and held her against a wall until his drugging kisses and the added intensity of his caresses had her crying out for more.

In the bedroom, he gently tossed her down on the bed and pushed away her hands when she went to help him disrobe. He finished the task himself, took care of protection and pulled her from the bed. He settled her sweetly once he'd cradled her bottom in his hands. He demonstrated his strength, taking her while standing dead center in the middle of the room without the aid of a wall or doorway to lean upon.

Misha was as aroused by his awesome show of power as she was by him guiding her slowly up and down the length of his shaft. She gasped over a moan when her nipples brushed the sleek pecs that tensed each time he drew her up over him.

She kneaded the mesmerizing hardness of his biceps. She couldn't close her hands around them. He ordered her to kiss him in that deep, beautifully accented voice of his. Of course she complied, moaning even as she obeyed. Faint slurping sounds accompanied her moans and she could feel the abundance of liquid streaming from her core.

Talib's hands tightened on her bottom. His climax was near but he wanted more from her, much more.

Misha felt the same. This was perfect, too perfect with the moonlight streaming softly past the blinds. The sounds of the wind hitting the chimes that surrounded the house and the sounds of their need swirled through the room. Misha clenched her fists against his broad chest and beat softly while succumbing to the effects of his very filling sex. He took her right to the edge, allowing her to dangle there before he tugged her over.

Misha woke early the next morning and decided to indulge in a little sightseeing on her own. Gingerly, she eased from the sheets and wrapped herself in the fleece blanket that had fallen to the floor during last night's encounter.

She didn't venture far from the house and didn't need to for what she had in mind. She enjoyed a devastating sunrise from the rear patio area. Her eyes misted and she knew it was a mix of her reaction to the beauty before her eyes and sorrow for the man she loved.

He'd been honest with her the way she'd wanted. Now

she couldn't be sure if he was better or worse for it. She couldn't even be sure if *she* was.

Talib carried so much guilt for the things that had happened. There was guilt that he couldn't erase and that he wouldn't allow anyone else to erase. Just where did that leave her and the story *she'd* yet to share? He would surely hate himself for what happened if she ever told him. As for removing the guilt from his heart, she could just forget about that.

But he deserved to know just the same, right? He deserved to know the reasons fueling her cautions about them jumping back into all the many levels of the sweetness they'd shared. He deserved to know, even if she wound up losing him just the same.

Misha felt his fingers in her hair and smiled, meeting the kiss he bent down and offered.

"May we share?" Talib motioned toward the blanket she'd wrapped around her otherwise nude body. He was just as nude.

Misha gave him a saucy look. "Why, what would Armelita say?"

Talib was tugging open the blanket. "She's seen it. Long story," he added when she laughed.

Misha quieted when he snuggled behind her and pulled her onto his lap. She could have melted onto him as love, warmth and a glorious vista fed her body and soul.

"Do I have permission to talk about last night?" she asked once a few moments of the renewing quiet had settled.

Talib's fingers began a devilish journey beneath the blanket. "Which part?" he murmured next to her skin.

Her resolve fled and seconds later she was twisting and rising to meet the provocative movements of his hand between her legs. "I'm trying to be serious," she moaned and then cursed her lack of willpower.

At last, Talib took pity. He removed his hand while urging her to have her say.

"I only want to know if you're okay." She turned beneath the blanket, resting her hands flat on the granite wall of his chest. "The conversation got so intense last night. I wanted to know everything but I hate that you had to go through that."

"I didn't hate it." He prodded her chin up with his thumb. "I didn't hate it. At the time, yes, but now I feel like a weight's been lifted, and I know that sounds clichéd but it's true." He smoothed his thumb across her chin and followed the movement with his ebony stare. "I've walked around so bogged down by that story and for so bloody long that I didn't know what it'd feel like to walk around without the weight." He nudged her forehead with his. "Thank you for bullying me into talking about it."

"It wasn't me." She raised her hands defensively. "You wanted to share it. You just needed a shove."

"You're right." He found her hand beneath the cover and squeezed. "I wanted to share it, should have shared it long ago. If I had—"

"Hey? Shh…" Hair slapped her cheeks when she

shook her head. "I won't let you do that. You took a huge step last night."

Talib laughed when she kissed him. "I'm trying to confide here, you know?"

"Well, I'm taking a page from your book, then. When faced with a subject you prefer not to discuss, kiss."

Talib's sleek brows rose as he considered the phrase. "That's a pretty good move, isn't it?"

"It gets better," she promised and plied him with another kiss.

Chapter 15

Talib took Misha back to her suite without much conversation along the way. He had the feeling she could use the time alone. He could probably use some himself. While he'd planned to share more with her during their trip, he never thought things would become so intense. But talking to Misha the way he had, no matter how emotional, had done him good. He felt drained, but in a good way. Perhaps now he could turn a more skeptical eye toward the guilt he'd saddled himself with for the better part of his adulthood. *Perhaps.*

"So what's gonna happen with Ducker and Blaine?" Misha asked when she and Talib were at the front door to her suite.

"We've arranged for a meeting at the office tomorrow."

"Do you feel good about that?" Misha braced back against the message desk near the door.

"Right now I do." He grinned. "Ask me again after the meeting."

"So…" Misha sighed when the silence grew a bit too heavy.

"We've got the event for the Arizona Orchestra and then our trip will be pretty much at its end," Talib shared, his dark eyes narrowing. "I'll let you rest." He kissed her cheek and left.

Misha spent the morning reviewing notes from the budget meetings she'd missed. Silently, she thanked Riley for keeping her in the know. After scanning the meeting minutes, she planned to get some editing done on pieces the rest of the writing staff had emailed.

Again, she gave thanks for the work. She needed all she could get her hands on. She wouldn't dwell on the fact that it'd take no less than a ton to keep her mind fully occupied and off of Talib Mason.

The bell rang and she slipped from the armchair. Outside there waited a smiling woman with a huge box in hand.

"*Bowtiques,* ma'am."

Misha stared blankly at the card the woman produced. Then, snapping to, she moved back from the door and granted her entrance.

"Excuse me, who…"

The young woman laughed. "I'm sorry, ma'am. We're

the dress-and-tuxedo shop on the corner. Will you need any help trying on your item?"

"Uh…" Misha blinked as the sales associate removed the box top. "No, uh, thank you." With tentative steps, she moved closer and gasped at the "item," a dazzling black satin creation. "No, thank you," she breathed, smoothing the back of her hand along the rose blush bow which ran diagonal from just below the bodice to drape the middle of the dress.

"There, um—" mesmerized, Misha rubbed the material between her fingers "—there must be a mistake. I didn't order anything. I'm just in town for business."

"Oh yes, ma'am." The young woman smiled bashfully. "Mr. Mason placed the order on his account."

Renewed interest brightened Misha's face. "Right."

"Have a good day, ma'am."

When she was alone, Misha whipped the gown out of the box and gave it a closer look. The dress was absolutely gorgeous. She saw the gift card lying within the silvery tissue wrapping.

From me, to you, for me.

She smiled and then she was stifling a moan in response to the tingle the suggestive words evoked. The ringing of the room phone offered a much needed interruption.

"Miss Bales?"

Misha was still scanning the card. "Yes?"

"Ms. Bales, this is Rita from Lorel Spa. We're just down the block and calling to confirm today's appointment."

Misha was wholly focused on the call then. "Rita…"

"Yes, ma'am, of the Lorel Spa."

"I see." Misha tossed the card back into the box. "Rita, was this appointment set up by Mr. Mason?" She smiled when the woman sounded as if she were actually giggling.

"Why, yes, Ms. Bales. Yes, it was."

"Misha. Good morning." Talib raised the mug he held. "Have some?" he offered, waving the cup so that the aroma of the coffee wafted toward her.

Misha blinked away from the slab of honey-braised chest visible beneath the folds of his hunter-green terry robe. "I came to thank you."

"Ah." Talib stepped back and waved her inside the condo.

"Lovely, but unnecessary," Misha said with a sigh once she'd strolled into the living room.

"Well, you can't very well go to the orchestra naked." He sipped the coffee and scanned her body. "Nice as that might be for me."

Talib set down his mug and walked over to where she stood leaning against the sofa. He leaned down to cup her face. "I did this because I wanted to, not because you're the type of woman who'd expect it or would *do* anything to arrange it."

"Okay." She felt completely stupid for momentarily thinking otherwise. She gave a curt nod and turned to leave.

"I can't wait to see how it looks." Talib smirked before Misha slipped out of the room.

Talib figured conversation should remain the order of the evening. He could barely think of anything other than touching Misha, which would only result in them going back to his condo (or her suite) and forgetting the night's charity event.

"Thanks for coming tonight, love."

"Isn't the limo a bit much?" She rubbed her hand across the gray suede seating.

"Trust me, anything less would be out of place with this crowd."

"At least the museum people know they've invited some deep pockets."

Talib glanced past the window at the glamour they approached. "The Arizona Symphony concert will donate its proceeds tonight to the Arizona-Sonora Desert Museum."

Misha whistled. "Deep pockets indeed."

Talib propped his arm along the back of the seat. "We've been a couple of idiots, Mish."

"I'd like to think we've grown a little recently."

He took her hand and began to circle his thumb in her palm. "We've probably still got a ways to go." He brought her hand to his mouth. "Maybe we could do it together."

Misha was skeptical. "Fate may have other plans, Tali."

"It often does." His probing charcoal stare was

trained on her elaborate updo that allowed none of her loveliness to be hidden. Appraising the fullness of her mouth, he leaned in to kiss her.

"They'll be opening the door in about two minutes, sir."

"That'll work," Talib whispered in response to the driver's announcement. His tongue outlined the pout of Misha's lips seconds before it invaded.

She melted the instant his tongue stroked hers. Limp, her fingers toyed with the lapels of his tux. She whimpered, feeling his expert touch investigating the dress—familiarizing itself with every snap or button of which there were few. She began to thrust her tongue hungrily against his.

Moments later, it was Talib pulling away with a hushed curse on his lips. He reached for his handkerchief and fixed the damage to her lipstick.

"You look like you've just been kissed," he said.

Misha took the handkerchief and wiped a bit of lipstick from his cheek. "Is it a good look for me?" she asked.

"The best," he confirmed, seconds before the passenger-side door opened.

The orchestra was superb and Misha lost herself in the music and the atmosphere. Talib had box seats to the event, which made the already exquisite experience even more captivating.

"This must've cost you a pretty penny," she whispered,

fidgeting some when she felt his fingers at her dress's split.

"Anything for charity," he replied.

The program ended to a round of uproarious applause. Several people spoke to Talib when the lights brightened and the audience began making its way to the ball that was about to begin below. Misha felt her head spin when he introduced her to everyone who shook his hand.

"So how'd the talk go?" she was asking later while they were swaying to an incredibly romantic, hypnotic piece of music.

A last-minute snafu earlier that day sent Talib into the office to mediate a conversation between Blaine and Ducker Conrad.

"It wasn't pretty, but it was effective."

"Do you think things will get better?"

Talib sighed. "Not from one conversation, but now the door's been opened." He toyed with the diamond stud in her ear. "I think they'll both step through it. Only time will tell whether they've got the guts to see what's beyond it."

Misha pressed her lips together and enjoyed the swaying of her body against his. His nose trailing her temple, the scent of his cologne and the hardness of his sculpted frame were things she could have lived on forever.

"What's happening between Blaine and Ducker...do you think the same could ever be true for you and your father?"

When a response to her previous question wasn't

forthcoming she continued, "Did you see him again after he left?"

"Like most *fathers* who run off, the bastard resurfaced after he'd heard of my attending school in America and doing well in football." His embrace tightened about Misha's slight frame. "He actually thought I'd be thrilled to see him. Said he'd always loved me but knew Mum would never let us have a real relationship with the way things ended."

Misha now regretted asking, knowing the story wouldn't have a happy ending.

"I thank God for my uncles being there when the bloke came calling. I got in one good punch before they pulled me off. I haven't seen him since. My uncles raised me just fine. Any guidance I needed, I got from them. They were all the father I needed."

"I understand." She nodded, pressing her hands to his face. "I understand."

He brought his head down to rest on her shoulder. "I was happy when my father was out of the picture, too," she said.

She stroked the silky hair tapering at his neck and remembered.

"My mother worked her ass off while he played 'man of the house,' drinking beer all day with his deadbeat friends. The best day of my life was when I got off the bus to find Mama waiting to take me to our new apartment." She laughed, but quickly grew solemn. "I often wondered if Daddy even noticed Mama leaving with our cases packed. I guess as long as she didn't take the TV, he was okay."

Talib tried to ease the tension. "I'd liked to have been a fly on the wall when the power was cut."

Their laughter mellowed into a wicked kiss mingled with more swaying to the sensuous music.

"Are you ready to go?" he whispered next to her cheek.

"Whatever you say, Talib."

"You're getting good at that." He grinned, nuzzled her nose with his and they left the crowded ballroom.

Chapter 16

Misha woke in a cloud of confusion. For a few moments she studied the fabric she rested on. Awkwardly, her nails grazed the suedelike deep burgundy material. Slowly, she pulled up and blinked to clear her blurred gaze. There was definitely too much celebrating last night, she thought.

The area was unfamiliar, but before she could grow uneasy, she saw Talib across the rather wide aisle separating them. He'd taken off his shoes, and propped his feet on the swivel chair opposite the one he occupied. He was awake and watching her with his arms folded across the now wrinkled shirt he'd worn beneath the tuxedo jacket that rested across her while she slept.

Suspicion blared in Misha's gaze as she studied his face, sexy with a satisfied smile while his head rested against the high back of his chair. She pursed her lips and looked on in hopes of gathering more clues about her surroundings and ignored Talib's content expression.

Hell, he should feel content following the very enthusiastic interlude they shared in the limo after the gala. She patted the bodice of her dress, taking note that it was in place. She could just recall wiggling back into it. Shifting on the seat then, she ordered herself not to even wonder where her underwear was.

Maybe that was best not remembered. Actually, there wasn't much she *could* remember. Then she felt the vibration beneath her feet and stilled, taking in the strange sounds that were also filtering through.

Talib settled deeper into his seat and watched Misha whirl around, raking back the scant curtains covering the cabin windows. He heard her cry out over the realization that they were several thousand feet above the ground. He moved over to peer out the windows, as well.

"That isn't New York?" she asked, already knowing.

"Better." He sighed.

"England."

Misha didn't fall victim to the subdued feeling she felt in Arizona. *This* was sheer disbelief. She'd traveled over Britain before en route to other destinations. But she had never had the opportunity to actually set down in the country. Now she realized that nothing could compare with the place as the holiday season approached.

At the jetport, baggage carts were decorated like

sleds with holly leaves at the corners of the windshields. Additionally, the drivers had fashioned holly wreaths about their caps. The change in temperature hit Misha like a slap in the face. She was shivering while wrapping herself more tightly in Talib's tuxedo jacket.

Talib was already muttering to himself, tuning into the fact that she was dressed totally inappropriately for the weather. He cuddled her against him and hurried across the tarmac.

The brief trip from the Hud-Mason jet to the waiting car turned Misha into a veritable icicle by the time she was bundled inside. Talib was apologizing profusely for neglecting her coat and brushed his lips across her forehead as his hands roamed her arms to instill warmth.

Talib was moving to prepare her a drink, completely oblivious, it seemed, to her stunned expression. Misha took the goblet of drink and downed it like a dying woman. The cognac coursed across her limbs and instantly heated her frozen state.

Misha had since remembered fully the night before— how Talib had spoke of England and how she told him she'd never been there, followed by his offer to take her there…immediately.

"Thank you." She closed her eyes in a delighted shiver. "Are you sure about this?"

Talib smiled softly at her question. He took the goblet with intentions to refill it. He shook his head while she rambled off reason upon reason why this wasn't the best idea.

"I mean, did you even call ahead to tell them—"

He turned and took her chin in a firm hold.

Misha felt too weary to post more arguments. Her lashes settled demurely. "Whatever you say, Talib."

A steady rain started shortly after their drive began. Talib explained they were heading into Winchester, located in the county of Hampshire.

"My uncles Baron and Cafrey live here."

"Why is it that you've got their last name?" Misha asked, tugging his jacket snugger about her shoulders.

Talib figured she'd be better off with her arms inside the sleeves and turned to assist her. "My uncles arranged for me to have the family name when my mother passed so there would be no legal confusion." He buttoned the oversize garment about her slight frame. "Legalities didn't matter much to me. I wanted no part of a man who didn't want me."

On impulse, Misha inched up to kiss his cheek. In response, Talib plied her with a more thorough kiss.

Year round, the town of Winchester boasted streets that were brightly lit for shopping. Tempting merchandise lined every store window. There were boutiques and galleries in addition to food markets with almost every delectable imaginable.

Misha's eyelids were growing heavy from the cognac she'd consumed in an effort to get warm, but she resisted giving in to drowsiness when there was so much to see. Already, evidence of the upcoming holiday season was in view, with storekeepers getting a jump on the frenzied shopping that always occurred as Christmastime drew near.

"This is always quite a sight." Talib squeezed Misha's hand while taking in the excitement beyond the windows. "But they begin preparing for the season earlier and earlier every year," he added with a look of mild disapproval.

The rumbling of his voice in her ear where she rested on his chest lulled Misha more potently than the drink. The ride continued with Talib pointing out every attraction: the city museum, the Hospital of St. Cross and the town's exquisite theatre. They were passing the waters of the River Itchen when Misha finally gave in and let her eyes close.

Baron and Cafrey Mason lived outside of town, but close enough to be considered residents, and highly-regarded residents at that. The two youngest sons of Kent and Mabel Mason grew up more interested in horses than politics, much to their father's disappointment.

Kent Mason was a local barrister who claimed an impressively lengthy list of minority clients. As word spread of the man's prowess for arguing cases, his client list diversified and his profits increased.

Still Baron and Cafrey were content in raising, racing and breeding horses. Much of the family thought them fools for not following in the family business on some level. Of course, no one could argue with the wealth and reputation the men had acquired when they followed their dreams.

Still, regardless of their accomplishments, the brothers' biggest assets were their hearts. Their love for family and friends was legendary. Therefore, it was no surprise to find the successful entrepreneurs waiting under large black golf umbrellas for their nephew's car to arrive at the gate.

Talib kissed Misha's forehead and left her dozing while he went to greet his uncles with hugs and kisses.

Housemaid Serena Nettles laughed merrily when Talib swung her high and kissed her cheek. "We need to get out of this rain before we all catch our deaths." She nodded toward the car. "You did bring your young miss, didn't you?"

Talib nodded and headed off to the car. The others followed.

"Why, she's just a little thing." Serena gasped when she peeked in at Misha, still fast asleep. "And what's this? What's that she's wearing?"

"We, uh, didn't take time to change." Talib cleared his throat at the triple set of disapproving glares sent his way.

"Let's get her out of this straightaway." Baron was reaching into the back of the car. "My Lord, she *is* a small one," he noted while pulling Misha close.

Umbrellas sheltered overhead as the group made its way into the house.

Misha rarely experienced embarrassment, yet when she opened her eyes she jumped in response to finding herself bumping against a strange man's chest as he speed-walked with her in his arms. She caught sight of

Talib's smiling face as he followed along behind them with two other unfamiliar people. She kept her mouth shut, thereby lowering her chances of making an even greater fool of herself.

"Misha, these are my uncles, Baron and Cafrey Mason. The busy lady rushing around you is Serena Nettles."

Misha nodded and exchanged smiles with the three people in the den. She thanked Serena, who bustled about removing Talib's damp jacket and replacing it with the beautiful black-and-tan afghan she'd taken from the back of the leather sofa.

The handsome older men next to Talib greeted her politely before sharing agreements on how lovely she was. The brothers did nothing to mute their appraisals, which had Talib softly chastising them while Misha blushed shamefully.

"Is the chill beginning to wane, love?" Baron moved close to pat her hand.

"We apologize for our nephew," Cafrey said while casting a disdainful look at Talib, "bringing you halfway across the world in an evening gown."

"I'm fine, really." Misha wouldn't acknowledge the cold still clinging to her bones.

"Let's get a little sherry into her system."

"Oh, no, please." Misha waved her hand toward Cafrey, already heading for the walled bar which occupied an entire corner of the room. "I think I've had enough today." She thought of the two goblets of cognac that aided in her passing out.

"We can't have you catching cold when we have so much in store for your stay."

Misha studied Baron closely. "How long have you known we were coming?"

"The squirt called the day before," Cafrey shared, tilting the decanter of sherry toward Talib.

Misha slid a glare in Talib's direction.

Perceptive to a fault, Baron and Cafrey noticed.

"Come now, dear, did you honestly expect the man to waste more time than he already has? The family's been dying to meet the woman he'll make his wife."

Misha just barely managed to hold on to the glass Baron set into her hands.

Later, with the fire blazing and a bottle of Bordeaux on the table before them, the brothers gave Misha more insight into the Mason clan.

Interests spanned law, business and politics. The latter, according to Baron, appealed to the flashiest members of the family who'd secured places within the government.

To Talib's embarrassment, the uncles pulled out photo albums. The pictures had Misha laughing heartily as she observed the man she loved during those awkward boyhood years. Serena brought in soup and sandwiches. Misha turned down the food and was promptly bullied into trying a little of the black-bean soup.

"Tomorrow we'll tour the lands," Cafrey shared, while adding pepper to the already spicy soup.

"Are you comfortable on horseback?" Baron asked.

"More and more comfortable every day, literally," she laughed. "I guess it was just a couple of days ago we were on horseback touring Blaine Conrad's property, right, Talib?"

"Blaine?" A grin spread across Baron's face when he heard the name.

"How *is* that rascal?" Cafrey asked Talib.

While the men spoke, Misha gave in to the yawns that had been demanding release for the last fifteen minutes.

"I think this lady needs her rest," Baron said as he noticed Misha yawn. "I can imagine you didn't get very good sleep slumped over the seat of a plane."

"Thank you all so much," Misha was saying when Serena arrived to escort her to a room. Cafrey and Baron each pulled her close for good-night kisses. Then it was Talib's turn.

He brushed his mouth across her cheek. "I'll be up shortly."

"You certainly *won't* be up shortly," Cafrey corrected rather loudly. "The little thing is worn out and needs rest, not to be pounced on by you."

Despite the weariness plaguing her, Misha had to laugh. So did Serena, while taking Misha by the arm and leading her from the firelit den.

The brothers turned off the charm when they were alone with their nephew. Cafrey slapped the back of Talib's head.

"What the hell were you thinking bringing her all

this way in an evening dress? She's nearly frozen to the bone."

Talib rubbed the area where Cafrey's hand made contact with his head. "I wasn't thinking, I admit that. Coats aren't things one thinks about often in Arizona. I'd planned for us to leave the following day, actually. I didn't think the opportunity to come would present itself so readily." He folded his arms over his chest and shrugged. "It was already late when we left the affair in Arizona…"

Baron hooked his thumbs around his suspenders. "Cunning," he noted.

"More like stupid," Cafrey argued.

"Are things still in such a state between the two of you that you can't be truthful with her, boy?" Baron asked.

"That's not it." Talib groaned into his hands. "Truthful is all I've been lately, finally."

Baron and Cafrey exchanged looks.

"I just need more time with her and I knew that'd be tricky in New York. Besides—" he waved toward them "—I wanted her to meet you both. I knew she'd want to, especially after what I told her…about Mum."

Again, the brothers glances met and their hearts softened towards their nephew.

"I knew that couldn't have been an easy story to tell." Cafrey walked over to rub Talib's back.

Talib didn't mind letting his uncles see the lost expression he couldn't hide. "You've got no idea."

"So what's the plan, then, chap?" Baron asked.

"You've told her of your parents, she'll be meeting more of the family during her stay. What are you hoping to accomplish?"

Talib massaged his neck and walked to the den. "She thinks she was beneath me and I…I think she may have always felt that way, long before things got ugly between us. I guess I made it worse then. Now I only want her to see that it was never about her not being good enough. It was about a lot of my other personal issues, but not that. Never that."

Chapter 17

"After all these years don't you think it's time you both tone down with that stuff?"

"All women like to be pampered, squirt. You young chaps could learn a thing or two."

Talib had been playfully scolding his uncles over their pampering methods while they enjoyed breakfast the next morning.

"It's not just us young chaps. The two of you make it impossible for any mortal man to live up to."

Baron and Cafrey exchanged mock toasts with their coffee mugs.

"Misha will expect this sort of treatment every day from here on out."

"Well, she should," Baron argued. "Women are to be treasured, tended to as properly as they tend to us."

"We men benefit from the care they give us. Why shouldn't we return the favor?" Cafrey challenged.

Talib grinned and helped himself to another spoonful of the smooth porridge laced with Serena's special blend of cream, honey and sugar. "With that sort of mission statement, you two should be old married men by now."

Cafrey shrugged. "It'd be selfish of Barry and I not to drench such good care on as many women as we can."

More laughter filled the dining room and was just silencing when Serena walked through the doorway. She was wringing her hands.

"Porridge is good as always, Serena," Talib commended.

"Thank you, love," Serena walked over to pat the back of Talib's head. "I went up to take a tray to Misha. She was still sleeping."

"Good. She needs it," Baron said. "I can only imagine how worn out she is."

"I went to tuck in the covers. She was burning hot when I touched her forehead."

Serena's words drew the men's full attention.

"I tried not to overreact—" Serena quieted when Talib dropped his spoon and rushed from the dining room. She turned to Baron and Cafrey. "I thought perhaps a second opinion might be best before we called Doc McCallum."

Moments later, all three of them were following the path Talib had blazed.

When they arrived on the second floor, they found

Talib standing just inside the bedroom doorway. He appeared uncertain, or was just plain unable to move any farther.

Cafrey smoothed a hand across his nephew's back and felt the young man jerk. He moved beyond the doorway with Baron right behind him.

"Call the doctor," Baron hissed to Serena once he and Cafrey had pressed the backs of their hands to Misha's face and neck.

"She's definitely taken a fever," Baron said.

"Jesus." Talib moved into the room finally and sought refuge in the nearest chair. Fists balled against his mouth, his dark eyes were narrowed and filled with anger against himself.

"Talib, son, this wasn't—"

"Don't, Uncle Caf." He slanted the men a terrible glare. "We all know that's a lie."

The brothers left Talib alone in the room shortly afterward to go wait for the doctor's arrival. Talib watched over Misha. His mind, though, was riveted on the scene six years earlier, with her lying in a similar fashion and there not being a damn thing he could do about it. And just like six years before, he was once again to blame.

Doctor Rory McCallum ran his quaint but lucrative practice from his home just inside the Winchester town limits. He only made outside house calls to a select few patients and the Mason brothers were a couple of them.

"She's a tiny one," Rory whispered while tucking the covers about Misha after he'd completed the exam. "It's a wonder the lad hasn't crushed her," he said jokingly in reference to Talib.

"How is she, Rory?" Baron asked once they'd all shared a laugh at Talib's expense.

"Well, it's definitely a fever." Rory mopped his freckled brow with a handkerchief. "Probably started a couple of days ago but the lengthy trip dressed the way she was certainly didn't help any. Ask Serena to keep her trussed up in these gowns, would you? I doubt Ms. Bales will find them fashionable, but the weight of the material will help her sweat out the fever." The doctor rolled down his shirt sleeves and turned to his friends. "I've given her a little something that should help, but I expect she'll have a rough day and night."

"Is there anything more we can do?" Cafrey asked.

Rory shook his head, green eyes twinkling as he looked back at Misha. "Keep her bundled. I doubt you'll get a good amount of liquids into her but that'd help. The fever could put her in a really bad state before it breaks. She may even start talking out of her head." He shrugged into his tweed coat. "It should break sometime during the night, but if it rises sharply or you're just plain unnerved by it all then give me a call and we'll arrange to get her to town."

The Masons thanked the doctor and were ushering him out of the bedroom when they found Talib lurking in the hallway.

"There you are, lad," Doc McCallum greeted with a broad smile.

"Doc." Talib moved to shake hands.

"She'll be fine, son," the doctor assured. "Fever's bound to put her in a bad way but I'm confident it'll break during the night."

Talib could only nod.

Baron saw Doctor McCallum out while Cafrey saw to Talib.

"It'll be best for one of us to keep a watch over her during the day and the night especially."

"Right." Talib agreed with his uncle, but didn't sound too keen on being one of the *watchers*.

"I know you don't want to hear this, squirt, but you can't blame yourself. What's done is past." Cafrey clapped Talib's back. "You should know that better than anyone. After all, isn't that what you're trying to get Misha to believe?"

Cafrey left the room without waiting for a response.

The day was indeed a rough one. Misha tossed during her sleep as she seemed to struggle to awaken before falling back into a deep slumber. Talib remained far from the second floor most of the day, gaining updates on Misha's condition from Serena. The woman had toiled away most of the day working to get juice or just plain water into Misha's system. Any urgings to get Talib to sit with the patient were met by stern looks and silence. Eventually, even the brothers stopped trying to prod their nephew.

Fate intervened when one of the mares went into foal that evening. The birth of a calf was cause for celebration at the Mason stables. Even Serena was busy providing hot drinks and cakes for the men who all oversaw the birth. Talib was left to watch over Misha for the evening.

Serena had already instructed him to work on getting fluids into Misha's system if she awakened. Talib wasted no time seeing to the task. Whatever unsettling thoughts raced his mind, nursing her back to health had to take precedence.

Misha was frowning and tossing amidst the covers. She clawed at the ruffled neckline of her gown, seemingly desperate to rid herself of the heavy material.

"Shh, love, it's all right." Talib soothed her while tugging down her hands and pressing kisses to her fingers. "Shh…" He added kisses to her damp brow and cheeks.

"Tali?" Misha murmured slowly, turning her face toward the sound of his voice.

Talib chuckled. "It's me, love. Shh…"

"Talib…"

"Honey, you need to drink something. It'll help." He was reaching for a glass on the nightstand.

"I didn't mean it, Tali. I didn't…"

Talib smiled, pouring water as he squeezed her hands. "Shh…you've done nothing wrong," he said, thinking she was referring to the fever she'd come down with.

"I didn't mean to…but they…they helped. They helped, Talib…."

His movements slowed a bit as he watched her more closely.

"They helped…."

His curiosity took over and he set aside the glass. "Who helped, love?" He smoothed moist tendrils of hair from her small, oval face, knowing this was probably the "talking out of her head" Doc McCallum had warned them of. Still, something drove him to knowing.

"The pills helped me…they helped…when you left…I didn't mean to—to let them…take over…"

Talib released her hand, lest he crush it.

Misha continued to murmur and Talib clenched a fist. The rage that he'd set on simmer for the day began to rumble, demanding full heat. He felt sick. Sick of himself.

Misha's tossing was appearing to wane as sleep set in once more. Dutifully, he tucked the covers up close around her neck and lingered near to kiss her temple. Then he returned to his chair and watched her from afar.

Once all the hoopla surrounding the new foal had settled, Baron and Cafrey returned upstairs. They announced the addition of a new gelding on the ranch, but didn't expect their nephew to be overly joyous.

Meanwhile, Serena was checking Misha's forehead and announcing that she felt cooler. As the three celebrated the possibility of the fever breaking, Talib gathered his things and excused himself.

Chapter 18

By morning it was official: Misha's fever had broken. Serena went to check in on her and found the patient sitting up in bed and pushing at the ridiculously long sleeves of the gown that was at least ten sizes too big.

The curiosity in Misha's dark eyes spoke volumes and Serena had to laugh. Taking pity, though, she settled down to explain all that had happened.

"Oh, God." Misha was mortified and covered her face with the big sleeves of the gown. "First I oversleep in the car, then I take sick and you all have to nurse me back to health." She flopped her hands pitifully at her sides. "Talib's uncles must think I'm quite the catch."

"They do." Serena spoke without hesitation as she fussed about the bed. "We all do, dear."

Misha shook her head. Clearly, she was a nonbeliever. "Where is Talib?"

"The poor thing." Serena's mouth curved downward. "He's been in such a state since you've been ill. He blames himself for bringing you all this way dressed like you belong on the Riviera."

"I should find him." Misha laughed.

"Oh, no, you don't." Serena tugged at the covers Misha tried to push away. "Not until you've had a proper breakfast, missy. I'm heading down to fix you a plate if those greedy beasts haven't cleaned out all my pots, that is."

"Are they having breakfast now? Serena, please." Misha sat up straighter. "I feel well enough to go down and eat. You won't have to come back up here with a heavy tray."

"They'll have my head if your traipsing around the house makes you sick again." Serena waved off Misha's plea.

"Come on, Serena, we both know who runs this house."

The woman's brown cherubic face began to glow with amusement. "You are a sly one." She wagged a finger.

"Please, Serena. I've been cooped up in here long enough."

"Humph. I do admire your spunk, missy." Serena clapped her hands. "All right, then, let's find you something more appropriate for the breakfast table."

"What a blessing to have Misha come out of her fever so quickly," Baron said while topping off his coffee.

Cafrey nodded. "Especially with everything going around these days. But she's a healthy little thing." He raised his mug for more coffee.

"We should send up our prayers. Her illness could've been worse—a lot worse."

"It'd do some of us good to remember that," Cafrey murmured.

Baron chuckled. "That can be difficult when some of us are idiots."

Talib slammed his fist to the table. He drew raised brows from his uncles but no comments.

Then Misha walked into the dining room and each man stood. Of course, the brothers rushed right over to welcome their houseguest.

"I swear…" Baron marveled, cupping Misha's oval face in his hands. "Even with that fever, you were a sheer beauty. Healthier now, you're even more remarkable."

"I couldn't have said it better myself." Cafrey kissed the back of her hands.

"You two are really overdoing it now." Misha rolled her eyes. "I know I still look a fright. I really must apologize for being so worrisome." She smiled when they both waved her off. "I asked Serena if it'd be all right to have breakfast together."

Before Baron or Cafrey could lead her to a chair, Talib was taking Misha's arm.

"Are you really all right?" He cupped her cheek as she nodded yes. He led her to the chair closest to where the uncles were sitting and reclaimed his place at the far end of the table.

"Doc McCallum will be over to check on you after breakfast, love." Cafrey set a plate before her.

"Thank you both for taking such good care of me."

"Talib was with you when the fever started to break," Cafrey shared. "His presence must have worked some sort of magic."

Misha peered at Talib through the heavy fringe of her lashes. "Thank you," she said, but silently she questioned the guarded quality of his dark gaze.

"We talked him into giving us a few more days with you, but we understand you're a career lady."

"Yes, I should really call and check in," she told Cafrey, imagining the messages that must be clogging her phone.

"Don't worry about it," Talib spoke up from where he sat. "I already called Riley and explained."

Misha nodded, still questioning his obvious mood. If she didn't know better, she'd swear he was angry with her. But why?

"So it's settled, then." Baron clapped his hands. "We'll give you the rest of the day and night to get yourself together. Then the rest of the family is demanding their chance to meet you."

"Oh…" Misha's fork paused over her eggs. "I hope you all haven't planned any big get-togethers?" She didn't want the rest of the Masons having any preconceived notions about her and Talib. Things were still up in the air. *Way* up.

"They simply wish to welcome you to the family, dear." Cafrey leaned over to rub her hand.

Another fist-slam to the table drew everyone's gaze and instilled silence. Misha looked away from Talib's stony expression. She kept her eyes lowered as he passed her on his way out of the dining room.

The rest of breakfast with Baron and Cafrey passed easily. The brothers were full of conversation and questions about Misha's work, which helped to keep her mind off their nephew. Still, Talib's brooding was a dark shadow that loomed in the back of everyone's mind.

Following the meal, Serena ordered Misha back upstairs and into a hot bath. Misha's mood improved drastically. A claw-foot tub right in her bedroom and before a raging fire was just too perfect on an overcast day in the English countryside.

Talib walked in while she was soaking up the warmth still left in the water and enjoying the sway of the tree limbs against the wind. Misha pushed up a bit in the tub, her ebony stare narrowed and expectant.

He sat on the black padded bench at the foot of the bed. Leaning forward, he bridged his fingers and held them between his knees. "Were you ever going to tell me?"

Bewildered, Misha shook her head. "Tell you what?"

"About the pills."

She paused. "How—?"

"You weren't yourself during the fever. Doc McCallum warned us that you might say strange things in the midst of it."

Misha blinked away and began fidgeting with a damp tendril of hair that clung to her neck.

"Were you ever going to tell me?"

"Why?" She looked up just in time to see his expression turn murderous. Boldly, she continued. "You're already blaming yourself for what happened to your mother, and *that* had absolutely nothing to do with you." She leaned back against the tub. "How could I tell you this and have you lay fresh blame at your feet? Besides, what purpose would it serve? It was in the past, nothing would have changed it."

"Yet you were all too interested in every aspect of *my* past."

"That was different."

"How?"

Misha slapped the surface of the water. "The pills were an aftereffect. The accident…it was a bad one. It took me a long time to heal." She hid her face in her hands when the memories rushed in. "I was in a lot of pain and out of work—I quit *The Beacon* after all that went down. So…" She flexed her hands around the sides of the tub. "Out of work, out of a man and in a lot of pain. The pills were a big help…or so I thought." She gave a pitiful smile. "I needed them for the physical pain…at first. Then, it was for all the other pain. Thank God for Lett."

Talib straightened, resting his hands to jean-clad thighs.

"She was there when I was finally able to open my eyes. She was the only one I wanted to talk to. I couldn't even face my mother. I've never said anything to Riley either about it, I was too ashamed. I only told Lettia about the pills when my dependency started to scare me." She shook her head and focused again on the swaying limbs beyond the windows.

"I believe *the reason* you blamed me for my supposed betrayal was because of all that happened between your parents." Her gaze was defiant then as she fixed him with a glare. "*That* was why I had to know."

Talib bowed his head and began to rub his fingers through the glossy curls covering it. "It didn't take me long to know you hadn't betrayed me."

"That's right. I *didn't* betray you."

"I know, and you're right. All the baggage I carried did play into how I handled it—or *didn't* handle it, actually."

"Lettia insisted on me seeing a therapist after I told her about the pills." Misha sighed, realizing that they had gone too far to hold back anything more. "Once I accepted that things were truly over between us I was able to get myself back on track. Then you started being nice to me and I panicked. What if we had another falling out and I was out and driving through another storm and got into another accident? What if I became a slave to those pills again?"

Talib left the foot seat and went to stand before the windows.

"Talking about those feelings helped a lot—it

still does. I don't feel weak for admitting that. Those thoughts…I sometimes have them but they don't terrify me like they once did. I'm not their victim anymore. Regardless of what happens in my life from here on out, I never intend to be a victim again."

Talib closed his eyes, silently thanking God for that.

"Talib?" Misha called when the silence lasted a bit too long for comfort.

Slowly, he turned from the windows. "Thank you for sharing that. I know you don't want me to feel blame, but I *am* sorry."

"Talib—"

"I'll let you finish your bath."

Misha wouldn't give in to the tears when he left her alone in the room.

Later that afternoon, Misha felt up to taking a walk. Once Serena had given her approval, she set out to see the new foal everyone had been talking about. She found the mare nursing her calf and Talib there watching them. She halted in the archway of the stable, unsure whether to stay put or back away.

Talib would let her do neither. "Come over here," he said, waving.

Misha kept her steps slow when she noticed the animals' ears twitching. She came close and knelt to observe in wonder.

"I've often wondered if we'd ever have one of our own." His voice sounded hollow.

"A horse?" Misha frowned.

Talib's dimples flashed when he grinned. "A little one—a child."

Misha felt her mouth go dry. She thought she couldn't be any more stunned.

"I, well, humph. Your family already has you making me your wife—I guess the next logical step is a *little one*."

Talib didn't find her joke amusing. "That was for real, Misha. I had every intention of proposing to you before we left England."

Her heart was in her throat. "You *had* every intention?"

"I understand why you didn't want to tell me about the pills. Now that I know…" He focused on the hay he worked between his fingers. "I have to think about all of this again."

"You mean reconsider," Misha clarified.

"I love you." He turned and shook his head in case she were about to doubt it. "I love you too much to risk…" He couldn't finish and rose to his feet.

Misha stayed put, her tilting gaze still trained on the horses. "I love you, too—too much *not* to risk it."

The muscle danced along his jaw when he tensed further. "But what if some other dumb stuff goes down again between us? You almost didn't survive it last time." He practically grunted, stroking his jaw when the words hit home. "I sure as hell wouldn't survive it this time."

"Could you stand not knowing where I am?" She

picked up a tuft of hay and slapped it against the sleeve of her sweater. "Could you stand not knowing how I'm doing...or who I'm with?" She met his gaze slowly when he whirled around to look down at her. "I lived through that already, Talib. Doing without you again just to keep things safe..." She grimaced. "It's a bad way to live. If given the chance, I'd prefer not going back to that."

Talib pulled her to her feet. "I wish I could promise you—"

She shook her head, placing an index finger across his mouth to silence him. "I don't want your promises. I want your love. I want *you*."

His tension seemed to wane. A smile emerged. "Well, I can certainly promise you've got that, Miss Bales." He bumped his forehead to hers. "You've damn well got that."

The words melded into the kiss he planted on her lips. Misha kneaded his arms beneath the suede fabric of his burnished gold jacket as she stood on her toes, seeking as much height as she could gain. She almost didn't even register that they'd moved from the stall housing the mare and her foal, until she was lying on a bed of fresh golden hay in the farthermost stall.

"Someone could walk in," she warned in a small voice when Talib's mouth trailed to the scoop front of her sweater.

He kicked the wooden three-quarter door shut. "They'll hear you before getting close enough to see us."

Misha laughed. "I like your confidence, Mr. Mason."

"It takes confidence to please a woman like you." He grew serious then.

Misha turned serious, as well. "A woman like me?"

He brushed hair from her face and followed the line of his finger as it curved her cheek. "Exquisite, sweet, to be treasured and mine—all mine."

Misha blinked, allowing a tear to stream from the corner of her eye.

"Don't cry, love," he soothed, the provocative glide of his accented voice bringing an added sensuality to the moment. "I love you, Misha. Through all the stupidity, I swear I never stopped."

"I never stopped, either." She shook her head, gripping the lapels of his jacket. "I love you, Talib, so much."

They sealed their vows with a kiss.

Chapter 19

The next two days were like a blur, but a most enjoyable blur as far as Misha was concerned. She'd met much of Talib's family and found them to be as down-to-earth as Cafrey and Baron. But none of them were pleased with Talib when he insisted on getting Misha back to New York. The group was, however, somewhat pacified when he promised they'd return shortly after the New Year.

Misha was adding a few final items to her suitcase when Talib stepped into the room, closed and locked the door behind him. She smiled when he encircled her in his arms and nuzzled his face into her neck.

"I should really be doing this." She gestured toward the suitcase then rested her head back against him and enjoyed the magnificent feel of his body behind hers.

"And I should really be doing *this*."

Misha saw the diamond ease beneath the line of her gaze. "Talib." Her voice was scarcely a whisper. "Isn't this…too soon?" She felt his laughter rumbling through her.

"It's been six years. Do you love me?" he asked in the same breath.

"So much." She nodded without hesitating.

"Will you be my wife, then?"

She turned in his arms, done with excuses. "Always." She bit her lip while he eased the ring onto her finger. "How do you think Riley'll take the news that she's about to lose her editor to the West?"

Talib's black stare narrowed and he tilted his head to peer more directly at her. "You'd really do that for me?"

The "little boy" awe in his voice tugged at her heart. "I love you. We've done without each other far too long. Being with you, wherever you are, means more to me than anything," she swore, loving him all the more when he appeared truly stunned that she'd begin her life again for him.

Moments later she was rewarded by a strong kiss. The yoga pants and zip hoodie she'd worn that day were soon only memories.

"Why am I always first out of my clothes?" she murmured while he undid her bra clasp with expert fingers.

Talib suckled her earlobe. "It's important to get to the good parts first."

* * *

"His head is buried in a folder and the phone conversation doesn't sound like one that'll be done in a matter of minutes."

Misha shook her head over Baron's announcement. "Well, I hope you both won't mind lunch with just me."

"We prefer it that way, love," Cafrey admitted, and sent his nephew's fiancée a sly wink. "Just clearing our conscience by making sure we made every effort to include the squirt."

Misha's laughter was full, even as a curious frown marred the area between her brows. "Talib's about as far from a squirt as you can get. Why in the world did you two ever start calling him that?"

Baron was already laughing. "He wasn't always that size, love, but a short, scrawny stick of a thing and *we* towered over *him!*"

"Then one day we looked around for him and found ourselves looking up, *way* up!" Cafrey bellowed while raising his mug for emphasis.

"That's my fiancé." Misha sighed the phrase and enjoyed a sip of her tea. Shortly though, she took note of Baron's and Cafrey's knowing smiles.

Baron didn't wait for her to inquire. "We like the sound of that word—*fiancé*."

"You've no idea how thrilled we are by it, love." Cafrey leaned over to pat Misha's knee.

"Brother, I'd say we aren't nearly as thrilled by it as the squirt!" Baron reclined in the armchair he occupied near the fire. "We've never seen our nephew more alive."

Misha smiled. "I can't take all the credit, though."

"If not you, then who?" Cafrey extended his hand in pretend outrage.

Misha was shaking her head. "Talib speaking out about the past was what finally did the trick. I know he loves me, but until he was able to share all that…hurt, we would've never had a chance."

Baron and Cafrey both nodded. Silently, each was giving in to their own regrets about the past.

"Olivia." Cafrey swallowed and bowed his head to massage his nose before continuing. "Talib's mother— she was the youngest of us."

"The youngest and the sweetest," Baron qualified. "We never wanted a day of unhappiness to touch her—we all felt that way." Like his brother had done earlier, it was Baron who bowed his head then to massage away the sudden pressure at the bridge of his nose.

"Damn it all if she hadn't taken the lot of the unhappiness," Cafrey murmured.

"Why didn't any of you like Talib's father?" Misha's voice was a whisper, barely rising above the snap and crackle of the fire in the hearth.

Cafrey murmured a curse. "The jackass was after her money. It was all clear as day to us, but he swept her off her feet."

"And looked good while he was doing it," Baron smirked. "Talib's the spitting image of the bastard."

"Libby had no intentions of taking money from us,

though, once she discovered how we felt about him. She told us she didn't need the money anyway—that her husband would do a fine job of taking care of her."

"Pity he didn't know his wife's expectations before he married her," Baron added to his brother's explanation.

"The bloke was ambitious, though." Cafrey picked at a loose thread on the arm of the tweed chair he held. "He figured he'd come out on top regardless. And by God if he didn't—came out on top fast and flashy... caught the eye of that pretty assistant of his."

"Humph, for a while."

Misha frowned toward Baron. "What happened?"

"Hell, she left him shortly after he walked out on Libby and Talib."

Stunned, Misha sank back into her chair. "How do you know all of this?"

The brothers exchanged sour looks.

"We'd been keeping tabs on all of them." Baron left his chair. "When Olivia started moving around we lost track...until she called asking us to take Talib."

"Why did this woman leave Talib's dad? She'd gotten what she was after—why walk away from it?"

Cafrey grinned. "If she were a man, I'd say because the chase was done."

"But?"

"Like we said before, the fool did everything fast and flashy. Shoddy may be a better word, actually." Baron shrugged. "It all fell apart in the end."

"Misha, most people don't understand the true meaning of hard work. It's that way for a reason. Hard means solid and lasting." Cafrey looked to his brother for confirmation. "The more easily it comes, the more easily it can fall apart."

"Davin Sorrels," Baron said, claiming a spot on the arm of the sofa, "Talib's dad, didn't get that part, but we think he may have gotten the hint later on."

"Does Talib know any of this?" Misha held her hands clenched to the sides of her slacks. She watched as both men shrugged.

"The last time we know Talib saw his father, we think he may've been too taken aback by seeing the man to pay close attention to how riddled the chap appeared."

"Frayed edges on his shirt," Baron explained, "frayed coat collar, shoes were dusty and beaten up. He must've taken to cutting his own hair."

Cafrey went to stoke the fire. "We made some inquiries and found out his business had fallen apart."

"I can't believe he doesn't know." Misha was still stunned and could scarcely shake her head over the matter.

"I'm sure Talib wanted nothing more to do with him after that visit." Baron watched the flames rage beneath the poker Cafrey rolled amidst them. "His life was looking up. He didn't want or need to be reminded of it."

"Besides, I think he'd have told us something." Cafrey had returned to his seat. "Especially once the man was in his grave."

"His grave?" Misha sat straighter. "Both of them… both of his parents…?"

Cafrey and Baron nodded in unison.

"Happened shortly after Talib went to the pros," Cafrey said. "We weren't about to bring him down with that news. If he ever found out, it'd have to be through his own investigating."

"You think us cold, love? For not breathing a word of it?" Baron studied Misha's face closely.

"I don't." She shook her head before staring down at her hands. "I don't, it's just… I think he needs to know it if he doesn't already." Memory carried her back to the Conrad Cove visit. "I think regardless of how he might deny it, he could have been open to some sort of relationship with his father. Whatever it may have been." She shuddered and moved to warm her hands around her tea mug. "Leaving that possibility open in his mind…it's not right."

"You know him best, love." Cafrey's brows rose in a skeptical manner. "But I know I don't have the strength to do it. Baron?"

Baron shook his head toward his younger brother and then toward Misha.

She'd known the chore would rest at her feet before the brothers even admitted their unwillingness to follow through on the task. Of course she had no desire to be the bearer of more ugliness when they'd already faced so much. But better now than later, she acknowledged while squaring her shoulders. She wanted it all behind them. She wanted no dark clouds from old storms looming over the happiness they'd been so blessed to find again.

* * *

Talib worked well past lunch from his Uncle Baron's study. There were only a mere two hours left before dinner but Misha decided that her fiancé could use a break. Therefore, she used that excuse, along with some of Serena's homemade oatmeal cookies and ale, to visit the study where she found him jotting notes and inputting data to his laptop.

"May I interrupt?" she called after knocking softly and waiting for him to look up.

The serious expression shading his features vanished like mist when he saw her. Waving once, he tossed his pen to the desk and leaned back to watch Misha walk in with the tray she carried.

"Need help?" he offered, smiling when she used her hip to bump the heavy door shut.

"I got it." She was just setting the cookies and ale on a clear spot on the desk when Talib tugged her to his lap.

"Thanks for that—" he slanted a stare toward the tray "—but I prefer this." He murmured next to her skin. His mouth was already trailing upward to nuzzle her earlobe.

Misha bit her lip, lashes fluttering uncontrollably as his touch affected her. For a few sweet seconds she allowed herself to forget why she'd come.

Talib's mouth was busy surveying the sensitive area behind Misha's ear. His fingers, meanwhile, conducted their own survey of the buttons along the cream cashmere sweater she wore. He'd undone several before her hand closed over his.

"You should have something." She made an airy gesture toward the cookies and heard his chuckles vibrate against her.

"That's what I'm interested in right now, love."

She moaned and unconsciously arched into his exploring touch. "You didn't eat."

"I will."

The growling intensity of the phrase had Misha thinking he was intending on something other than food to dine upon. She pulled at his hand.

"There's something I want to talk to you about."

Slowing his moves across her skin, Talib's expression regained a little of its earlier seriousness.

He cupped her chin, preventing her from looking elsewhere. "What is it?"

"I'm always coming to you with something ugly." She felt his hand tighten on her hip.

"Are we in trouble again?"

Misha's heart melted when she heard the uncertainty laced within his deep voice. Quickly, she shook her head and brought her hand to the side of his face. "It's not that. No, we're fine. We're fine, I swear it." She kissed his forehead and temple while rubbing her fingers through his hair.

"This is about your father."

The worry had eased from Talib's face, only to be replaced by a grim line across his mouth. Misha tensed as well, feeling his body grow rigid beneath the black knit turtleneck he wore. She expected him to bolt away as he often did when the conversation wasn't to his liking.

Instead, Talib reached for one of Serena's cookies and tapped it to the saucer. "What about my father?"

In spite of her earlier eagerness to tell him of the man's demise, now Misha hardly knew how to broach the subject.

"I was talking to your uncles over lunch and they told me…"

Talib smirked, watching as the crumbs dropped from the cookie he bumped along the saucer's edge. "They know, don't they?"

Misha paused. "Your father is dead." She frowned. "You know. You already knew."

He took a bite of the cookie and shrugged. "I haven't known as long as my uncles probably have. I found out a while ago, well after everything that happened between us." He set aside the cookie and grimaced.

"I was so angry. I wanted someone to vent it on and dammit if he wouldn't have been the perfect recipient." Propping an elbow to the desk chair, Talib braced his chin to a fist. "I was always curious about him, especially after he'd come snooping around when he discovered I was playing ball in school." He laughed. "I should have known those two old goats knew."

"Don't be angry with them, Talib." Misha grabbed a handful of his sweater and gave a tiny jerk, hoping she hadn't unwittingly driven a wedge between the men.

"They didn't want you to hurt anymore. You were doing so well then, moving on happily with your life."

Talib kissed her cheek and drew Misha more snugly into his lap. "It's fine, love. I'm not angry. I know they did it out of love. I love them as much for keeping it as I love you for feeling the need to share it."

"I'm sorry anyway." She watched him kiss her finger adorned by his ring. "I didn't want to bring it up when we're so happy finally. I just kept thinking of what Blaine said about Ducker, about seeing hate in his child's eyes. When we were out there, I wondered what was going through your mind then."

"Blaine said that before. Many times. I don't think he's aware of how many times I've heard it." He rested his head back against the chair. "When I was starting to make a name for myself, I often thought of ways I could go and twist the knife on my father. Make him regret walking away from us—away from me." His dark eyes slid to Misha's. "Then I heard Blaine say that and I knew my father had seen that very hate Blaine talked about. And then there wasn't anything more I needed to say or do to the man." He shrugged. "The hate he had to see lurking in *my* eyes was enough."

"Talib—" Misha brought her forehead to his "—I'm sorry." She smiled when he gathered her close. "I love you so much. I honestly don't know whether I could stand up under all the curves your life's taken you around."

"You know I'd take every one of them again if they led me back to you."

Misha curved her hand about his when he hooked it around her neck. Their kiss was brief, yet desire filled every second of it.

"I hope this is it," she sighed, closing her eyes on the wish. "I hope we're done with the heaviness, the sorrow..." She looked at him. "What you said once about things being left unfinished between us—are we finished now, Talib?"

Again, he squeezed her hip. "Almost." His expression was soft. "There's one last thing I need to share with you before we leave."

Misha cringed. "Is there more sorrow and heaviness involved?"

He grinned. "Somehow I think this time will be different." He patted her thigh. "Get your coat."

The silence in the pickup truck Talib had driven seemed to intensify once he opened her door. There was no eeriness, but peace. It was a peace that echoed in Misha's heart. She felt it in her soul as well and it became yet another emotion to add to that lengthy range of feelings she had been experiencing lately.

She curved her hands tightly into the crook of Talib's arm. That was as much to ward off the brisk chill in the air as to steady her feet along the walk through the cemetery.

When they stood at Olivia Helena Mason's grave, Talib released Misha's hand. Slowly, he knelt before his mother's headstone and carefully set the overturned vase upright.

Misha clasped her hands and watched him remove the dead leaves and weeds that had gathered near the base of the stone. He brushed the back of his hand across the engraved marble slab as though he were caressing it. Misha knew he was seeing his mother then.

"Mum, there's someone I want you to meet." His sniffle was followed by a laugh. "You've, um you've heard me speak of her often. I know it's nothing short of a blessing now that I'm finally able to bring her to you as my fiancée. Next time we visit, she'll be my wife." He turned, holding his hand up and out to Misha.

"This is Misha Bales." He made the introduction once Misha was stooped down next to him.

Misha couldn't restrain her tears which rushed forward the moment Talib had silenced. "I'm sorry, I didn't mean—"

"It's all right. It's all right, love." He drew her close and kissed the top of her head.

Misha composed herself, brushing at the tears streaking her face. Inching closer, she smoothed her hand across the stone as Talib had done earlier. "You've raised an incredible son," she spoke in a quiet yet undeniably strong voice. "He's a phenomenal man and I've always loved him. With everything inside me, I promise to take care of him this time—to treasure him always." Sniffling, Misha pressed the back of Talib's hand to her cheek before she kissed it.

Together, the couple sat embraced and speaking softly to the woman who rested below the ground.

Chapter 20

Francheska Bales had been floored by Talib Mason from the moment her daughter had introduced her to him years earlier. When things turned unfortunate for the couple, Francheska always believed the love was still there. While urging her daughter to move on with her life, Frankie told her that if it was meant to be between her and Talib it would be so in the end.

Francheska had had faith in the words but knew it was the desperation to pull her daughter out of a sorrowful well that fueled them. Realizing now that they had been true filled the woman with a hope she'd never dared to rely on.

"I really wish you'd let us take you out, Ms. Francheska." Talib leaned down to kiss the woman once

Misha had finished hugging her. "Have you waited on the way you deserve to be."

"Oh, you." Francheska slapped at the sleeve of Talib's shirt even though she appreciated the offer. "Tonight I prefer us to dine in a real setting. That way I can observe without distraction."

"Are you trying to see if we're for real, Ma?" Misha teased, smoothing the pleats of her black skirt beneath her while curling next to Talib on the sofa.

"Oh, no, baby, I can see that easily enough." Francheska placed three glasses of lemonade on the doilies on the coffee table. "I'm happier than either of you can know. Talib, baby, Misha told me about your parents. I am sorry, hon."

"Thanks, Ms. Francheska." Talib squeezed Misha's hand and smiled. "I don't think I'll ever stop missing my mother."

"A mother can never be replaced. Neither can a father." Francheska nodded toward her daughter then. "I don't think I'll ever stop regretting the fact that I let Mi Mi come up without a father."

Misha shook her head. "We were fine, Mama. I never felt that I missed out on anything."

"But it was rough and I feared it may have jaded you when it came to love."

"Ms. Francheska, it wasn't Misha's upbringing that jaded her, it was me."

"No, hon, I won't let you do that," Frankie argued.

Misha chuckled. "Don't waste your time, Ma. The man's got a thing for taking the blame."

"Well, it ends now." Francheska smoothed back the tendrils of hair left dangling from her French roll. "There will be no more apologies. You two have been through enough. The last thing you need is constant apologies hanging around to remind you of the things that drew you apart."

"Thanks, Ms. Frankie." Talib accepted the forehead kiss from his soon-to-be mother-in-law.

"And now that we've got that settled—" Francheska clapped her hands before resuming her seat and propping her slipper-shod feet to the edge of the coffee table "—talk to me about where you two are gonna live."

"Your daughter plans to pick up and come where I am." Talib shrugged as though he still couldn't quite believe it.

"As it should be." Frankie eased a wink toward Misha before moving to kiss her cheek. "It's a good decision. And when may I expect my grandbabies?" She laughed awhile when Misha sputtered into the lemonade she'd just taken a sip of and Talib's face went beet-red.

"Mama…" Misha chastised while pressing a napkin to her chin.

"What?" Francheska's light brown eyes widened in outraged innocence. "You're not gonna tell me this vibrant lookin' thing next to you doesn't have some thoughts on the subject?"

"There'll be as many grandbabies as she'll help me make, Ms. Frankie." Talib chuckled as Misha blushed profusely and her mother clapped loudly.

"Well," Frankie said on a sigh, settling hands to her

lap in a show of contentment, "I can tell this will be a blessed union full of love, full of cherishing."

Talib took Misha's hand then. "You've raised an incredible daughter, Ms. Francheska. She's a phenomenal woman and I've always loved her."

Misha bit down hard on her lip, recognizing the words that mirrored the ones she'd spoken at his mother's graveside. Her gaze blurred as he continued.

"With everything inside me, I promise to take care of her this time, to treasure her always."

Francheska Bales sat beaming with happiness and pride as the couple embraced before her.

No one could dispute the fact that Cache Media knew how to throw a party. The fact was thoroughly emphasized the night Cache celebrated the collaborative effort put together by *The New Chronicle* Sports Department and *The Stamper Court* on the biggest feature of the year.

The headline read Hud-Mason—New School Game, Old School Success. The exposé was a true surprise for Talib. After all, he had only conceived the story idea to aid in providing him more time with Misha. Asher, on the other hand, thought his partner's idea, no matter the motive behind it, had great merit. He'd also agreed with Talib that more exposure wouldn't be a bad thing.

Between the sports department, Riley and her team of writers, not to mention Misha, who had been instrumental in pulling it all together, the four-part series had printed under a great deal of anticipation. Despite strong circulation numbers, *The Chronicle* celebrated its best profits in well over a year.

"I fear we won't see this party to its end," Talib warned his fiancée.

The celebration was held at a popular Brooklyn dance hall which specialized in jazz and reggae. Misha knew he was as affected as she was by the pulsing music and lyrics.

"Maybe we should sit out the rest of the set?" she proposed.

"Not a chance," he growled into her neck as he massaged her back and bottom with sweeping strokes across the cherry red of the snug jersey dress she wore. "Exactly how did you have time to take part in this, anyway, with all the running around we've been doing?"

"I needed a mental escape," Misha confessed as their dancing slowed. "Especially while we were in Phoenix. It helped when I couldn't stand mulling over all our drama anymore. Besides, I wanted to be a part of this, no matter how small the part." She linked her arms around his neck and scanned their dark, sultry surroundings. "When Asher told us what he wanted, I had to find a way to make it happen. Pooling assistance between the two departments gave it all a broader appeal, greater hype. Not to mention the bottom line for Cache—greater profits."

"And here you thought my idea was a load of bunk."

Misha raised a brow in response to his taking credit,

and then she waved it off. "I had to be part of it if it was for you. If it hadn't been for *your* idea, who knows how all of this would have turned out?"

"I don't want to think of it," he said, wincing as the words met his ears.

Misha toyed with the collar of the denim shirt hanging outside his slacks. "That makes two of us," she whispered, and stood on her toes to meet his mouth as it descended upon hers.

Soon after, they began to sway to the music's affecting rhythm.

"I agree with you, love," Misha murmured into Talib's neck. "I don't think we'll see the party to its end."

Epilogue

Somewhere over the atlantic

Laughter rumbled low and content in the compact yet elegant rest area at the rear of the Hud-Mason jet. Basking in the aftermath of a beautiful sexual interlude, Talib and Misha cuddled amidst tangled coverings.

"I want to marry you tomorrow," Talib confessed, entwining his fingers between Misha's.

"Tomorrow?" She pushed up to watch him in surprise.

"Calm yourself," he soothed, maintaining his focus on their fingers. "That's not where I'm taking you. Besides, the uncles would have my ass if I were to bustle you through some quick arrangement when they've made all those plans."

Misha braced up on her elbow. "What…what plans?"

Talib angled an arm behind his head and casually filled in his fiancée. Baron and Cafrey Mason had planned a lavish fairytale wedding for the couple.

"They can't…" Misha swallowed, refusing to let a bout of speechlessness claim her. "I can't let them go to all that trouble. Your uncles are very busy men—way too busy to be planning a wedding." She could have laughed.

"Sorry, love, but from what I understand, it's all set. They've even delivered the plane tickets to Ms. Francheska." Talib referred to her mother.

"What?"

"Two days ago, I think."

Misha had no choice then but to laugh.

Talib shrugged, still maintaining his casually playful demeanor. "It's all part of the pampering process I'm sure my uncles have patented." His bottomless dark eyes traveled every inch of her oval, honey-toned face. "According to them, every bride should feel like a princess on her wedding day." He gave a one-shoulder shrug. "Who am I to argue such logic?"

Misha was still giggling, but quieted when he fixed her with a serious look.

"Are you okay with it?" He reached up to stroke her cheek with his thumb. "I only want you to be happy."

"You've already accomplished that."

Talib moved up to kiss her slowly. "I love you," he said as his mouth descended upon hers.

"I love you," she voiced as she reciprocated the kiss. Then, suddenly, Misha paused.

"We're going to England now, aren't we?"

"You've got that right," Talib said with a smirk. "But don't worry, I've packed enough clothes for you to make it through the entire winter without ever repeating an outfit."

Misha smiled and leaned in to plant a tiny kiss on Talib's nose.

"Whatever you say, Talib. Whatever you say."

* * * * *

Fru·gal·is·ta [froo-*guh*-lee-stuh] *noun*

1. A person who lives within her means and saves money, but still looks good, eats well and lives *fabulously*

REQUEST YOUR FREE BOOKS!

2 FREE NOVELS
PLUS 2 FREE GIFTS!

KIMANI™ ROMANCE

Love's ultimate destination!

KROM11